NIGHT OWL

girls'
ADVENTURE
stories

Copyright © MCMLXXXV by World International Publishing Limited.
All rights reserved.
Published in Great Britain by World International Publishing, Limited.
P.O. Box 111, Great Ducie Street, Manchester M60 3BL.
Printed in the G.D.R. SBN 7235 7742 0.

CONTENTS

THE
FORBIDDEN VALLEY

"Whew! What seamanship!" exclaimed Derek Grant as the tourist boat nosed its way through the rocky approach to Bergen Harbour. His companion, tall, fair-haired Karin Bryant, nodded.

"It gives me a thrill each time I come to Norway," she said.

The two had met on board ship crossing the North Sea. Derek, who intended hiking in Norway and staying at youth hostels, had been gratful for all the advice Karin could give him. It was his first trip abroad, whereas Norway was Karin's second home. Her mother, a Norwegian, had met Karin's father during the war when his plane had crashed on a Norwegian mountain. After their marriage they had lived in England, and now Karin's father was a test pilot; but every summer Karin spent her holiday with her mother's sister in a farm set high in the Norwegian mountains in the shadow of a glacier and an expanse of snowfields.

As the boat docked, Karin remarked, "Now for customs — a mere formality for us."

"Thanks for everything," said Derek. "I hope we meet again. Anyway, I'll take your advice and stay at farms wherever possible."

As they made for the customs-shed a burly, pompous man jostled against Karin, jerking her handbag from her grasp and stepping heavily on her foot. Derek retrieved her bag and glared at the man. Then the glare was wiped off his face. He smiled and said: "I hope you have a good holiday, Mr. Delamore."

The man stopped, and Karin, nursing her aching foot, waited for his apology. But instead he growled rudely, "Didn't know you were coming to Norway, Grant. Keep to the coast. Better for lifts." And, scowling darkly, he went on.

"He's one of the bosses at our lab," murmured Derek. "A super-brain."

"Oh!" said Karin testily. "Manners, however, aren't his strong point. And don't keep to the coast. That's what every tourist does. Go high up the mountains and see real Norwegian life."

"Rather!" promised Derek. And, shaking hands, they parted, Derek to explore the friendly, fascinating town of Bergen, and Karin to board a fiord-steamer that would take her to the isolated hamlet where she would be met by her aunt and her cousins Aase and Giske.

Listening to the lilting Norwegian chatter of her fellow-passengers, Karin felt excited and happy. As the tiny steamer chugged its way through the dark fiord water, turning and twisting into narrow rifts in the lofty cliffs beneath snow and ice, Karin wondered what news her cousins would have for her.

It was late afternoon when the ship's siren blew a shrill blast, the sign that they were approaching a village. Then round a bend appeared the village of Mordal, where Karin would leave the steamer. The small landing-stage was crowded, since the villagers met the steamer which called twicc weekly, when the water was free of ice. It was an event which they honoured, whether they had friends on board or not.

Karin soon spotted Aase and Giske in the little crowd. They waved excitedly. Then, on the road leading to the mountains, she saw her aunt seated in the family *stolkjaerre* — a wooden horse-drawn cart-like vehicle used in the mountains. Karin was one of the first to cross the gangway and, having greeted her formally with Scandinavian curtsies, the girls hugged her vigorously.

"Welcome, Karin. Welcome home," said Giske.

"It's been a long year," said Aase.

Seizing her cases, they hurried her to the *stolkjaerre*. She curtsied to her aunt, and then kissed the red, weathered cheek.

"Welcome, child," said her aunt. "My sister, your mother, is well?"

"She is well, and sends her greetings," said Karin as she climbed on to the wooden bench in the back of the *stolkjaerre*.

Her aunt rallied the dozing horse, and, leaving the tiny village, they turned up the mountain road, which rose in hair-raising bends above canyons and a rushing river to the rocky plateau which was the summit.

They were crossing a small stone bridge when a

luxurious car hooted imperiously behind them and, hogging them aside, took the road ahead.

"The English from Olaf Trygusson's *saeter*," said Giske grimly.

"English?" Karin stared, and glimpsed, seated behind the chauffeur, the hateful Mr. Delamore.

"They are not all English," said Aase. "In the village they say that most of the men there are Poles, Czechs and Germans."

"It matters not where they come from," replied Giske crossly. "The valley is forbidden to us. We cannot pick the blueberries and raspberries there this summer."

"That is gossip," said her mother reprovingly. "The gentlemen have rented the valley for the fishing and the hunting this summer. You will be able to pick berries at the mouth of the valley where they are not shooting the reindeer."

"There are only tame reindeer on Olaf's land," argued Giske, "and those are not for hunting. And everybody knows there are no fish in the lake below the glacier."

"And we know it is forbidden to pick the fruit," said Aase. "We . . ." she began, and stopped nervously.

Her mother negotiated an awkward bend successfully. Then she turned to Aase and said, "We will give the horse a rest here, and then you, Aase, can finish what you began saying."

Having pulled into the side of the road, she turned expectantly to her daughters. Karin glanced

at her cousins. They were blushing furiously. So Karin politely studied the view of the distant fiord lying beneath the snow-capped peaks.

Then Giske said: "It was the day you wanted raspberries for jamming, Mother. We went to the good place by the little waterfall at the beginning of Olaf's land, where we've always picked berries. We soon filled our buckets." She stopped, and Aase took up the tale.

"Two men, with a great dog like a wolf, came up to us. One spoke to us in Norwegian, but we were sure that he was not a Norwegian. He asked us who had sent us to spy. I said that nobody had sent us, and that we had always picked the berries in the valley. Then he spoke to the other man in a language we couldn't understand."

Here Giske interrupted, saying, "It was not English. You know, Karin, that we learnt enough English in school to understand even if we cannot speak it well."

Karin nodded worriedly.

"And then?" prompted their mother.

"Then the first man told us to go and not return. The dog growled at us. I think he would have attacked us, but he was on a chain. They took us up to our land," continued Giske, "and watched us leave."

"So," said their mother as she guided the horse back on to the road. "You must keep away from Olaf's land this summer."

As they climbed slowly to the top of the pass

Karin pondered over what her cousins had said. Then she remembered how Mr. Delamore had rudely told Derek to keep away from the mountains. It was all very mysterious.

When they had reached the rocky plateau which topped the steep ascent they could see their house in the distance. It crouched in the shelter of rocks, while above it the grim mountains towered. Around, the peaks glistened with their caps of eternal snow, and between the peaks a glacier thrust its green arms, veined with dark crevasses. The polished log walls of the old house shone in the pale sunshine, and its turf roof was weighed down with slabs of stone against the onslaughts of the great mountain winds. But inside it was snug. Double window-panes kept out the cold, and kept in the heat from the lofty wood-burning stoves that stretched from floor to ceiling in every room. It was a happy house, and as soon as Karin entered she forgot the sinister strangers of the forbidden valley.

The girls helped to prepare the evening meal. Then the outside silence was broken by the tinkling of many bells.

"Father has come with the goats," said Aase, smiling at Karin.

Running outside to greet her uncle, Karin was engulfed by goats. There were white, black and brown goats; nannies and billies, staid old goats and frisky kids. Her uncle had brought them down from their scanty pastures to be milked and fed.

The following days were typical of life in the summer in the Norwegian mountains. The girls helped with the household chores. They picked the wild berries for jam, and milked the goats morning and evening.

One sunny evening, as the two girls were diligently milking the goats, Giske said suddenly: "Look! Father's coming with a stranger."

Aase and Karin straightened their backs and turned to stare.

"Whoever it is, he's lame, and Father's carrying his rucksack," said Aase.

Suddenly Karin exclaimed: "Why! I know him! It's Derek Grant. We met on the boat coming from England."

"Go quickly," said Giske. "We will finish the milking."

As Karin ran towards the house, which Derek and her uncle had entered, she grinned as she remembered how she had told Derek to make for the mountains. He'd evidently taken her advice, and got into trouble. Then it struck her that her uncle and Derek had come from the direction of the forbidden valley. Had Derek been seeking Mr. Delamore?

Entering the kitchen, she was amused to see Derek seated at the table with a cup of neglected coffee before him, while he, frowning heavily, thumbed his way through a phrase-book. Derek was evidently having language difficulties.

"Can I help you?" asked Karin primly. Control-

14

ling her giggles, she thought she sounded exactly like a well-trained English shop assistant.

"English!" exclaimed Derek thankfully. Then he looked up, and, seeing Karin, said, "What a break! Am I glad to see you!"

He tried to stand, and winced.

"What's wrong with your foot?" asked Karin.

"Sprained my ankle on the mountains. It's lucky that this gentleman, who must be your uncle, saw me limping along. How far am I from a youth hostel?"

Turning to her uncle and aunt, Karin explained that she knew Derek and that he wanted to go on to a youth hostel.

"Nonsense!" said her uncle. "See to his foot, Karin. He has a small tent, so he must camp here until his foot is right. Youth hostel indeed!"

Later, when she had bandaged his foot and he was eating a hot meal, Karin asked Derek, "Were you trying to get to your friend Mr. Delamore?"

"Delamore? Is he up here? And he's not my friend. He's one of my bosses. A mere dogsbody like me wouldn't dare seek out Delamore outside lab routine work."

Then he became serious.

"Apparently," he said, "I trespassed this afternoon. I thought the mountains were free for all, and I wanted to get up near the glacier. I meant to camp there tonight."

"Yes," prompted Karin gently.

"I was getting along quite nicely, when suddenly

a mighty big alsatian swooped on me, and got me to the ground." Derek grinned sheepishly. "In fact I thought I'd been attacked by a wolf."

"And then?" asked Karin, leaning forward.

"Two men came and called off the wolf, I mean dog, and began gabbling in what I vow was German. I don't speak German, but once I worked with a German refugee, who used to talk to himself when an experiment went wrong. These men sounded just like old Hans in a rage."

"Didn't you try to explain?" asked Karin.

"I told them 'English'. Then one told me in broken English, 'Go. Mountain forbidden.' So I scrammed, and fell on some scree."

Sighing, Karin told him how some visitors supposed to be English, had taken the valley for the hunting and fishing.

"And Delamore is there?" asked Derek incredulously.

Karin nodded.

"He may fish, though I doubt it," said Derek thoughtfully. "But he certainly can't shoot. I remember him saying so when on a firm's outing we went to a showground shooting-booth for a lark."

"Perhaps he's wearing L for Learner," grinned Karin.

But Derek was serious. At last he said slowly, "You've made me curious, Karin. I think I'm going to drop in on that valley again. Delamore isn't the type to go in for fun and games."

"You won't be able to go anywhere for a week

or so, with that ankle," remarked Karin.

"No. But when I am mobile again, are you game to come with me? You know the lay of the land."

There was a moment's silence broken only by the plaintive bleating of the goats outside. Then, nodding briskly, Karin said, "I'll come. And I've just remembered there's another little-known entrance to that valley. I'll tell you later. But not a word to my family. My aunt would forbid it. And say nothing in front of the girls — they understand English. I don't want to get them into trouble with their mother."

For the best part of a week Derek nursed his crocked ankle. One day, as they sat outside his tent with their backs against a boulder, Derek said suddenly, "Pretty rocky that valley of Delamore's isn't it?"

Karin grinned.

"This part of Norway," she replied, "is mostly rock — where it isn't fiord, mountain lakes, and ice and snow. It's a relic of the Ice Age."

"Yes. That Ice Age. Very old, and very modern too," said Derek pensively.

"You speak in riddles, friend," said Karin lazily.

Then a humming noise overhead brought her to her feet.

"A helicopter!" she exclaimed. "I've never seen one here before."

With narrowed eyes Derek watched the machine. Then he sat up, saying, "Isn't it heading in the direction of Delamore's valley?"

"Yes."

18

Derek got up carefully. Testing his foot, he said:

"I think my foot could do with some exercise now. Let's go down to the fiord-village tomorrow. If my ankle stands up to the walk there and back I'll be able to do our jaunt into the valley."

Karin frowned. "Why rush things?" she asked.

"Because the time-factor is chancy; and we don't know how long the key men will stay up there," said Derek, more to himself than to Karin.

"Time factor? Key men?" asked Karin bewildered.

"I may be wrong, Karin. But Delamore's presence is giving me ideas. That little company in the valley may be on to something that's important, and dangerous in the wrong hands."

"You've been reading too many thrillers," scoffed Karin. "I loathe the man, but what harm can he do in an isolated Norwegian valley?"

Shrugging his shoulders Derek said, "Forget it. But promise to guide me in, please."

"I have promised, and I'm just as inquisitive as you are."

The following day the two set out for the village on the fiord. After a little stiffness Derek said that his ankle improved with every step. Once in the village they made for the village shop which was also the post office, as the sign with the postman's horn above the door showed. To Karin's surprise the chauffeur who had driven Delamore up the pass was collecting mail and speaking to the postmistress in German. She curtly handed him a bundle of letters, and when he had gone said to Karin, "I cannot be polite to Germans. You know, Karin, my Nils died at their hands in the Resistance."

Karin nodded gently. Then she said: "He's from Olaf's valley, isn't he?"

"Yes. There are all kinds up there — English, Poles, Czechs, Germans, and maybe Russians."

"Are there many English up there?" asked Karin.

"Only the one who rented the land from Olaf," was the reply. "He wrote from London. He must be rich, because they have a helicopter and a seaplane which lands on the lake by the glacier."

On the homeward climb Karin and Derek discussed the situation. Derek was anxious to leave for the valley early next morning, while the mist still covered the mountains, and so their movements would be less easily seen.

"Could you find the way in thick mist?" he asked.

"It would be tricky," replied Karin. "But I know the danger spots. But a better idea would be to leave my aunt's late in the afternoon, and stay the night in the refuge hut which is near the secret entrance to the valley. Then we would be fresh and more alert if we meet trouble."

"How secret is this way in? And do you think it will be patrolled?"

"I'm sure it will not be guarded because they wouldn't expect intruders from that direction. And it is really secret. Only the real mountain people know of it. It's a kind of ladder."

"Ladder?" exclaimed Derek.

Karin laughed at his dismayed expression.

"Not a wooden affair, but a series of steps hewn in the rock-walls countless years ago, before a road into the valley was ever dreamt of. It's difficult, and could be dangerous. But I'd rather risk a track I know than meet a ferocious dog that I don't."

"There's something to be said for that argument," grinned Derek. "I don't fancy being pawed and smelt by that beast again."

"A climb in the mountains will do you good, Karin," said her aunt next day as she packed two rucksacks with provisions for Karin and Derek.

"I hope aunt's right," muttered Karin to Derek. She felt excited and also scared at the adventurous prospect ahead of them. In addition to his rucksack, Derek carried a climbing-rope wound round his middle. This was Karin's idea.

They began their adventure in bright sunshine. Excitedly they climbed steadily, passing through moorland bestrewn with boulders and ice-green lakes; then they passed through a rocky canyon. Finally they reached a wilderness of bare rock with expanses of last year's snow in its hollows. Above, mountains of sheer rock with their peaks capped with snow encircled them, and within walking distance a glacier thrust its green arm menacingly towards them.

They had been silent for a long time. Then as Derek stared in dismay at the pathless desert of rock, Karin whispered as if afraid to break the silence: "There's the hut."

The refuge was anchored to boulders with strong wire cables, and its roof held down by huge slabs of stone. Derek followed Karin towards it. It consisted of two small rooms with four bunks in each. One room had a huge cast-iron stove laid with logs ready for lighting.

"Get snow in this pan while I get the fire going," said Karin. "Then I'll make the cocoa."

The warmth from the log fire and a meal of cocoa, sardines and crispbread followed by fruit, relaxed and refreshed them. Then, sitting in the glow from the fire, they discussed their plans for the morrow.

"We must leave about four in the morning," said Karin, "when the thick mist will give us good cover."

"Tell me more about this ladder," suggested Derek. "You've actually used it?"

"I've been down it twice with my uncle," said Karin. "I'll go first. You'd better rope me to you in case I slip. There are twenty-seven steps, and some may be slippery. So the going will be slow."

"I can't help thinking of that dog," Derek remarked uneasily.

"I should think it will be chained up at that hour," comforted Karin. "Anyway the dogs are probably used to guard the lower entrance where a regular path enters the valley. However, if we're caught we must say that we're lost."

"Too true," grinned Derek. "We'll be lost all right if we're caught."

"When we reach the bottom of the ladder," continued Karin, "we go right, towards the *saeter*. After that it will depend on what we see. What do you expect to see, Derek?"

Derek shrugged. "Men at work," he said, "and not good old English workmen, either. What about the road back?"

"I hope to pick up a path between the lake and the glacier. It's roundabout, but it leads eventually to the ladder."

Bolting the door, they took turns to sleep two hours at a time, so that they would be sure of an early start.

After a hasty breakfast they got ready. They were travelling light, taking only the rope, some chocolate, raisins, and an apple apiece in their pockets. Derek gazed longingly at some goat-cheese and crispbread that Karin replaced in her rucksack.

"No," she said firmly. "There'll be plenty of good water and wild berries."

Derek grimaced. "No diet for a growing boy," he teased.

"Come along," said Karin severely.

They slipped out of the hut, and walked in single file with Karin leading, into a blanket of mist. A cold wind blew off the glacier, and both were glad of the anoraks with hoods they had borrowed from Aase and Giske.

Visibility extended only a couple of feet ahead, and their progress was slow. Suddenly Karin stopped at what seemed to Derek to be a bottomless cauldron of mist.

"Rope," she whispered.

Deftly Derek roped them together, grateful for the training he'd had on an Outward Bound course.

"Here we go," muttered Karin. "I wish us luck!"

Derek smiled bleakly.

Intent on their descent, they had no time for fear. Both mentally counted the steps, and both sighed with relief when they reached the twenty-seventh. Some steps had been slippery, and Karin, who knew the depth of the rugged drop below them, had several uneasy moments.

As they rested at the foot of the stone ladder Derek suddenly saw a light flicker nearby. Gripping Karin's arm, he pointed. The light shone palely in the mist.

"House," whispered Karin. "Come on. Hold my coat."

Slowly they walked through heather. Then they heard the soft lapping of water, and Derek knew without being told that they were near the glacier's lake. They were almost upon the light when Karin stopped abruptly, and crawled on all fours into a rocky hide-out, pulling Derek after her. This natural rocky refuge had only one opening, and this gave an excellent view of the light. The mist was thinning, and Derek could see the outlines of two buildings.

Suddenly the mist lifted, and the farm-house door opened. Two men with a dog on a chain came out. Karin felt Derek stiffen. Fortunately the wind carried their scent away from the animal, and the men led him down towards the lower entrance of the valley. Karin smiled, and Derek gave a thumbs-up sign.

Shortly afterwards two other men came out carrying equipment. Derek narrowed his eyes, and nudged Karin violently. Moving clumsily with their burdens these men climbed the rocks above the lake towards the glacier.

Putting his mouth to Karin's ear, Derek asked, "Can we stalk them?"

Karin hesitated, scanning the landscape. Then nodding, she slipped out, and ran noiselessly on the blueberry plants, flitting from boulder to boulder. Derek followed her closely. The strangers were now ploughing their way over scree below the glacier. Karin and Derek realised that they could not attempt to stalk them any farther because there was no cover, and the small flints clattering beneath their feet would betray their presence. So, huddled beneath a rock, they waited and watched. A tinkling noise puzzled Karin. She turned to Derek with lifted eyebrows.

"Geologists hammering for specimens," he whispered against her ear, "I've seen enough. Let's go."

Karin shook her head. "Can't. They're in our way!"

26

At that moment a throbbing noise surged up the valley. It was followed by a seaplane, which in a matter of seconds landed on the lake. So intent were Derek and Karin on this that they forgot the geologists until they heard them clatter down the scree towards the lake. They were soon joined by more men from the buildings, among them Delamore. When they were all engrossed with the occupants of the seaplane Karin tugged Derek's arm, and whispered, "Quick!"

They dashed from cover to cover to reach the paths around the glacier, known only to reindeer and Norwegians.

It was a nightmare flight, and both were breathless when Karin stopped, and sinking on to a rock panted, "We're safe."

For a few minutes neither spoke. Then Karin asked quietly, "What do they expect to find in their rock specimens – gold?"
f the man's signals and promised him a good tip if he would take the three of them to the Rue Blanc.

Grimly Derek said, "No. My guess is uranium. And since there isn't a Norwegian amongst them, I think they mean to smuggle their finds out. To what country? Your guess is as good as mine."

"But that's stealing," gasped Karin.

Derek nodded. "And Delamore is a traitor. Let's get out. Where's our ladder?"

Karin was thoughtful as she led the way to their rocky staircase. They had reached its foot when, with a menacing throb, a helicopter hovered above them. Instinctively they both hid their faces and flattened themselves against the rock-face. But though the machine disappeared the way it had come, and was evidently off route, they both knew they had been seen.

Derek looked at Karin's white face.

"At least," he said, "they can't land here. The rocks are too close."

Mechanically they climbed up the stone steps. Once at the top they hid again in a circle of boulders. Then, deciding all was well, they came out into the open. Immediately, with its sinister hum, the helicopter returned. Petrified, they stared at it, and at the man descending from it. Then they saw that he carried a gun.

There seemed no escape. Still, Derek yelled, "Run. Dodge."

For a second Karin seemed stunned. Then in a low voice she said, "Follow me. Wherever I go."

Then she ran, zigzagging between boulders towards the ladder. But instead of going down, she swerved left where the rocks were close together. Half conscious of a mighty roar, Derek followed her. Round a bend they came up against an immense three-armed waterfall.

Over her shoulder Karin asked, "Can you see him?"

Derek looked behind carefully, and gasped, "Not in sight."

Karin looked up at the empty sky. They seemed safe from spying eyes.

"Now follow," she panted, and plunged straight at the middle waterfall. For a split second Derek hesitated. This seemed madness. Then he too ran into the fall. To his surprise he found himself in a small cave. Hidden under the middle fall was a protruding rock, so it was possible to dash under it, and enter the cave without getting wet.

Inside the cave the outside light filtered greenly through the water. Talking was impossible because of the roar of the three torrents. Standing beneath their curtain of water they waited for their pursuers. Their wait was short. Two men, both armed, came along the track, to be brought up sharply by the impassable cataracts. They searched every available cranny, then, shrugging their shoulders and shaking their heads, they turned back. One pointed significantly towards the canyon below. He evidently thought that Karin and Derek had fallen into the forbidden valley down below.

Shaking with reaction and the creeping cold, Karin rubbed some warmth into her limbs. Derek produced his packet of raisins, and then a bar of chocolate. But the cold mountain water cupped in their hands was more refreshing than either. They became stiff and cold, so they marched solemnly up and down, and round and round their tiny refuge.

It was not until nightfall that they felt it was safe to leave. Once outside, Karin tugged at the rope round Derek's waist. He understood, and roped them together again. Then, climbing over stunted shrubs, they gained a path that wound up and

30

above the waterfalls. It was rough going, and in places they had to crawl on all fours.

Suddenly a great silence hit Derek's ears. Then he realised that they had left the waterfalls far behind.

"Hello, pal," said Karin hoarsely. "A rest and chocolate, I think."

Gratefully they sat down under a sky brilliant with stars, and munched happily.

"Where are we?" asked Derek at last.

"On the mountain below the glacier which faces our house. In distance we haven't far to go, but we must skirt a snowfield, testing every step as we go. One slip would mean cold storage for keeps!"

"You've been a grand leader," said Derek self-consciously.

"It was pleasanter doing it by daylight with Uncle," confessed Karin. "But anything is better than playing hide-and-seek with that helicopter. Let's get moving."

Neither would ever forget the rest of the journey. Several times Karin stumbled, and once she fell into a snow-hole, to be hauled out quickly by Derek.

At last they came to a rough path.

"The worst is over," said Karin gaily. "We're on a goat-track that leads directly home."

"What's that light?" asked Derek. "There! Oh, it's hidden by a bend. There it is again."

Karin giggled hysterically.

"Now, we've had everything! It's a search-party."

Now, though bone-weary, the whole adventure seemed to have been fun. Cheerfully they yodelled to their friends below. But Karin had another surprise when the two parties met.

A tall, slim man stepped forward in front of her uncle and her cousins.

"Daddy!" yelled Karin. "Gosh! Who sent for you?"

"Nobody, Puss," he replied. "I was testing a new plane, and thought I'd join you."

Introducing Derek, Karin said, "And Daddy'll know what to do about Delamore and company."

"We had better get home," said Giske. "Mother has worried. She feared that Derek's foot was poor again."

So it was over an immense hot meal that they told their tale, with Giske, helped by Aase, translating quickly for their parents.

Karin's father listened intently.

"You are sure of your facts?" he asked Derek.

"Sure!" spluttered Karin. "If you think we dreamt up those geologists, and that beastly helicopter, and those gangsters with guns!"

Meanwhile, Derek, grinning at Karin's outburst, managed to nod to her father.

"Fair enough! I know a chap in Oslo who'll know what to do."

So that afternoon security forces closed in by land and air on the forbidden valley. And since spies can claim no protection from their masters, the fate of the men who had rented Olaf Trygusson's land created no diplomatic situation.

Later, Derek returned to his lab work, but Mr. Delamore did not. It would be a long time before he would be free to leave an English prison.

THE TOYSHOP MYSTERY

"It's snowing," said Sally Baxter delightedly, looking out of the office window into Fleet Street, where the early-morning traffic was making its way through a flurry of white. "Isn't that marvellous? The country will look lovely. It may even be cold enough to skate."

"By which I presume you have got a Christmas holiday while the rest of us slog away on duty? Ah well; we can't all be beautiful brunettes."

She grinned at the other junior reporter, who was leaning with an elbow on his typewriter in an attitude supposed to register despair.

"Come off it, Ian. I know perfectly well you are having your break at New Year so that you can go back to Scotland," she said. "And you don't intend to work particularly hard for the *Evening Cry* between now and then. Just one party after another while I go out on this perfectly awful assignment for the 'People who work at Christmas' series. The news editor has let you off while I. . . ."

"Let me guess. Deliver mail? Or sweep the streets?"

"Nearly as bad. Sell toys at Marshaws."

"So that's why you are wearing your little black frock?" the boy teased. "I thought you had joined the canteen staff."

Sally glanced at her watch and began to gather up her notebook and pen. As one of the few teenage reporters in the national newpaper office she was used to being teased, and even the note of jealousy in Ian's voice when he talked of a Christmas holiday did not worry her.

Although no newspapers were published on Christmas Day, there always had to be a skeleton staff on duty in Fleet Street and for the past three years she had been among the unlucky ones who had worked. This time, however, she was to finish early on December 24th and travel down to join her mother in the country at Nashbridge.

But before then she had a job to do. Don Howe, the news editor, had scattered his staff round the country doing the work that the Christmas rush entailed.

"You will go to that snooty store in the West End and sell toys, Sally," he had decided. "Write a human story about what it feels like to be a salesgirl. Aching back, tired feet. . . . You know the kind of stuff I want."

He had never spoken truer words, thought Sally later that day as, bewildered and flushed, she tried to master the art of selling teddy bears and dolls to the hundreds of harassed mothers and fathers who milled round her.

The other members of the sales staff had tried to tell her as much about the job as they could, but time was short. It was just a question of keeping her head and her temper as she struggled to wrap up parcels which just refused to come up to the Marshaw standard.

"I never was much good at mental arithmetic," she muttered to herself as she dashed over towards a till. "How much is £9.50, £6.99 and 15p! I am sure I could have done it if that child hadn't insisted on wanting a 15p balloon as well as a doll and a cot."

"£16.64," said a quiet voice by her side, and after Sally had handed over the parcels and the change she stopped by the side of a girl who sat at a desk, recording some figures in a book.

"Thank you. I keep getting into a flap. Never worked so hard in my life," she panted. "Perhaps I could break off now and go for some lunch. I wish I could look as calm as you do instead of getting hot dashing round the counters."

"And I wish I could dash around," the girl answered, with a sudden smile which brought a blush to Sally's cheeks. She had not noticed until that moment that one of her new friend's legs was held stiffly in front of her, with an iron brace clamped round it.

"I'm sorry," she said quickly. "I hadn't a clue. . . . Was it polio?"

"Yes, but I am used to it. Marshaws are very good. They have given me this sitting-down job numbering the parcels. You see, that is my grandfather over there."

Sally looked across the desk and spotted a familiar, white-whiskered figure.

"Santa Claus! Why, I have been too busy to notice him. There's been such a crowd in this corner I could not see what was going on."

The lame girl's eyes twinkled. "He has a 'post office' there. After people have bought toys the parcels are weighed and I write names and addresses on them. The parents pay the cost of the postage, and then the children 'post' them in Father Christmas's sack. It's a tremendous thrill for them because, of course, they are all delivered to their friends by reindeer."

"I would have loved it myself," Sally confessed. "Well, the crowds have certainly thinned off now so I will report to the supervisor and see if I can get some lunch. I want to write down some of my impressions before I pass out completely."

By the end of the afternoon Sally found that she was getting the hang of the job and began to enjoy herself as she bent down to catch the whispered requests made to her by children or tried to find exactly the right toy for some of the rich customers whose families appeared to have everything they wanted.

Occasionally she found time to check some of her calculations with Mary Inman, the lame girl, and to spend a minute or two watching the children 'posting' their parcels in Father Christmas's sack. She was relieved to know that the packages would be re-wrapped before they went to the real post office, otherwise some of her own bundles, she thought, would never reach their destination.

By the end of the day, after she had gathered some facts and figures to add to her article, she was weary.

The giant luxury store had closed its doors for the night and the tired assistants were streaming out of the staff doorway into the snow.

One by one they punched the time-clock, said goodnight to the doorman, and disappeared. For the first time Sally realised what the Christmas rush really meant for those who had to work in a shop and she felt she would write a glowing article about them which would touch the hearts of the *Evening Cry*'s readers.

In front of her she could see Mary Inman limping slowly down the corridor with her grandfather who, now stripped of his scarlet robes and beard, looked a fragile old man.

Thinking she would like to say goodbye and thank the girl again for her help, she hurried to join them. But a sudden burst of angry shouting from the doorman, who had been joined by two of his colleagues, stopped her.

To her dismay she realised that something was wrong. The sack which the children had filled and re-filled during the day with their parcels lay on the floor. In the doorman's hand was a small brown-paper parcel, which he had ripped open and was brandishing towards the old man.

Two men in lounge suits joined the group and Sally could see that deep distress was written on the faces of Mary and her grandfather.

With her reporter's instincts aroused, she went forward to join the group. Mary turned to her, tears streaming down her white cheeks.

"What on earth has happened?" she asked the stricken girl. "Is your grandfather in trouble?"

Everyone seemed to be speaking at once, but eventually one of the supervisors turned to Sally, with a fastidious shudder.

"I am sorry you have seen this, Miss Baxter," he said agitatedly. "Of course, these things never happen with our regular staff but when we have temporary workers there are isolated cases of theft. This man, our Father Christmas, came to us with the highest references but the doorman spotted him carrying his sack out of the building, rolled up under his arm. Just as a precaution he took it off him and shook it. This parcel fell out — and you will see what it contains. A dozen very expensive gold wrist-watches."

"But I didn't know it was in the sack. I had no idea. . . . I know nothing about it."

Sally's heart was touched by the absolute sincerity in the old man's voice.

"Why were you taking the sack home?" she asked gently, and Mary replied.

"There was a tear in it . . . and grandfather thought my mother would sew it up so it would be all right for tomorrow. She is a dressmaker. We are not thieves."

There was dignity in the girl's voice and even the irate supervisors seemed impressed.

Sally felt a quick urge to do something to help.

"You can't solve this problem tonight. Mr Inman is very tired and shaken. Can't you just keep the watches and sort the whole thing out tomorrow? I am sure there must be some explanation."

The head supervisor wavered.

"Well, of course, we should not like to read anything in the *Evening Cry* about this. Marshaws never get their name in the paper that way . . . and we are all anxious to get home before it starts snowing again."

"Then let's call it a day," said Sally briskly, feeling that the situation was going her way. "I have my car on the staff parking ground. I'll run the Inmans home and you can start your questioning again tomorrow."

The car was new and the girl reporter felt that she would never again use it for a sadder errand. The girl was quietly sobbing and old Tom Inman seemed stunned by the accusation that had been brought against him.

"I thought the sack was empty," he moaned. "All the parcels the children posted had been emptied out and their numbers corresponded with the check Mary had made in her book. I don't know where those watches came from . . . I really don't know."

Sally was convinced she could believe him, and when she sat in the tidy little sitting-room at the Inmans' home, she sensed that she was among good people.

"You see, my mother is a dressmaker," said Mary quietly, as she limped across the room to uncover an electric machine. "Ever since I was ill she has taken in sewing to help to keep us. My father died two years ago, and the three of us live together."

After Mrs Inman, who seemed as stunned as her father-in-law at the bad news, had made a cup of tea, Sally tried to collect her thoughts, although her head was spinning with fatigue.

"Now, let's think how the parcel of watches could have got into your sack," she said practically. "It was very small. Could one of the children have 'posted' it by mistake, do you think?"

"It wasn't addressed," broke in Mary. "So it didn't go through the same drill as all the other packages."

Sally leaned forward quickly. "Were all the parcels put into your sack by children?" she asked the old man. "Do you remember any grown-up 'posting' that packet?"

Tom Inman's eyes brightened. "There was one woman, just before closing-time. She put something into my sack and I asked her if she had had it weighed and addressed. She said something to me in a sort of foreign voice. I couldn't understand what she said. The next minute she was lost in the crowd and there were so many children clamouring for their turn, I never gave it another thought."

"What did she look like?" asked Sally, urgently.

He could hardly remember, Father Christmas told her, but had got the impression that she was tall and dressed in a short fur jacket and a light skirt.

"She wore one of those bracelets with a lot of odds and ends dangling from it. I remember that because it caught in the top of the sack and she snatched her hand away quickly as though she was angry about it."

Sally drove back to her lodgings very slowly, through the slushy streets. She knew she had left sorrow behind her at Christmas-time and was determined to try her best to cure it.

She would not be able to enjoy her own holiday if the thought of sadness at the Inmans' home was nagging in her mind.

Although she would gladly have crawled into bed after having her bath Sally had to sit down at her typewriter to create the article needed for the next day's *Evening Cry* about her experiences as a toy salesgirl at Marshaws' exclusive store.

It was not difficult to write, for, she thought ruefully, she still had the headache, backache and footache the strenuous day had given her. But she had not expected to have heartache as well, yet that was what she was experiencing, as the thought of Mary Inman's tear-stained face and the trembling hands of the old man kept coming back to her.

Tom Inman had taken such a pride in his job, she remembered. He loved children and knew just how to talk to them in the role of Father Christmas. To feel that even at the age of seventy he could get work, Mrs Inman had told her, made him happy, but now, despairing and suspected of theft, or collusion with a store thief, he was a broken man.

She glanced at the calendar. December 22nd. There was only one more working day before she could put the cover on her typewriter and travel to Nashbridge to start her Christmas break. Could she possibly do anything, in that one day, to help the Inmans?

Acting on impulse, she picked up the telephone and gave the Fleet Street number. Instead of taking her article to the office the next morning, she would dictate it to one of the typists who was on duty all night.

The man typed the words she read out as quickly as she could speak. At the end she asked him to leave a message for the chief reporter.

"Am returning to Marshaws in the morning instead of coming into the office. Story broke just as I was leaving which I want to follow up," she dictated. Then she went to bed feeling a little easier in her mind.

The people at Marshaws seemed surprised to see her before opening-time, for she had arranged to work on the staff for only one day. She explained that she had not come to sell toys but to absorb a little more atmosphere and see if there was any news about the watches.

On the surface, everything looked just the same as on the previous day. Father Christmas was settling in his corner with his sack, and a girl was waiting to address the parcels for the little children to 'post'. But both were new store assistants hurriedly transferred to take the place of Tom and Mary, who had been dismissed on suspicion.

Sally was soon hard at work on her investigations. In a departmental manager's office she learned that the store detectives were puzzled about the mysterious parcel of watches.

"We came in very early this morning and checked our stock of that particular make of Swiss watch. As far as we can see, none is missing from the jewellery department," confessed the head detective.

"Then Tom Inman did not steal them from you," Sally said quickly. "Surely that clears him and he can return to his job?"

"It partly clears him, but we cannot overlook the fact that he was taking valuables off the premises in one of the firm's sacks," said the manager in an outraged voice. "The whole thing is highly suspicious. What was he doing with the watches, we should like to know? Until he confesses we cannot have him on our staff, or his granddaughter either."

Sally sighed. "Have you been to the police?"

The men exchanged glances and the manager cleared his throat.

"No . . . not yet. Perhaps after the Christmas rush we shall have to report the facts, but you know, Sally, Marshaws have a very high reputation. We try to avoid any scandal if at all possible. As the watches do not appear to be our property, we shall keep them in a safe place for a few days to see if there are any inquiries."

"And in the meantime the Inmans will have a miserable Christmas unless I can do something about it," Sally thought as she wandered back into the store, which had just opened its doors to the public. She stood watching the first customers coming out of the lift on the toy floor, a stream of determined shoppers wanting to miss the rush which would come later.

Suddenly her heart beat a little faster. Crossing the floor towards Father Christmas was a tall woman in a short mink jacket over a beige frock. Her sallow face and brown eyes seemed anxious as she paused by the red-cloaked figure.

The new Father Christmas looked nothing like the one who had been on duty the day before.

Tom Inman was a slightly built, small man with twinkling blue eyes. The man who had taken his place was much taller, with a hooked nose and dark eyes.

Sally walked over to stand beside the woman and she drew a sharp breath as she saw a bracelet heavy with gold charms jangle on her wrist. This was the stranger Mr Inman had described the night before.

She was speaking now, in broken English, to Father Christmas, who was bending to catch her words.

"I have only just come on duty, madam," he said. "The man who was acting as Santa Claus yesterday is not here today."

Sally felt delighted that the woman seemed disturbed at the news and was glancing over her shoulder rather wildly as though she were looking out for someone.

Being a reporter on a national newspaper had often meant playing amateur detective. The girl had to think quickly of some way she could identify the woman and link her with the parcel of watches.

But before she had time to make a plan, something happened with dramatic suddenness.

The woman, who was already pale, had gone deathly white and her eyes glanced round the store as if she wanted a way of escape. She muttered something under her breath.

Sally, watching keenly, realised in a flash what had caused the mink-coated figure to panic. A swarthy man, with dark glasses, wearing a heavy waterproof, had come into the toy department and was making his way through the crowd of shoppers towards them.

Her reporter's instinct told her the woman wanted to get out of his way.

Quickly she turned to the stranger and in a low voice said, "Do you want to leave the store, madam? If you will come with me I will take you to the lift."

The gloved hand, with its jingling bracelet, clutched her arm.

"*Merci*. I feel faint. . . . I must get into the open air."

Sally pushed her roughly through a door marked "Private", which she remembered from the previous day led into a corridor used by the staff.

The service lift, luckily, was standing unattended, and in a second she and the woman she judged to be French, or French-speaking Swiss, were descending to street-level at the back of the building.

The woman leant against the wall saying nothing, but showing signs of agitation. She closed her eyes, only opening them when the lift came to a halt.

"This way," said Sally, walking towards the staff exit, where she explained to the doorman that a customer felt ill and wanted to go out.

"I'll get you a taxi. There is one on the rank at the street corner," said the man, putting his finger in his mouth and giving a shrill whistle. When they were inside the cab, with the woman still looking anxiously around to see if she were being followed, Sally asked where she wanted to go.

"The airport. Quickly."

The words gave the girl a shock, but her reaction was quick.

"What a coincidence, madame. I am going there myself. I was just killing time in the store," she said. "My plane leaves before lunch."

"To Paris?" the woman said nervously. "That is lucky, for we can share the taxi. I am very fortunate to have met you. You are going to France for Christmas?"

"No. Just on a business trip, returning almost immediately," improvised Sally, realising she had no luggage to back up her story and hoping her handbag looked bulky enough to contain her night things. But the woman was too worried to notice details, and when the taxi reached the airport she clung to Sally as though she wanted moral support as they went into the reception lounge.

The stranger, once inside, seemed anxious to lose her, but Sally was determined to ignore her wishes. "Let's have coffee," she said briefly, leading the way to a table.

The woman looked across the lounge and said abruptly, "Do you speak French well?"

"I wish I did. No, English is my language," Sally answered, thankful that she did not have to tell a deliberate lie as her French was, in fact, quite fluent, a fact she obviously was not prepared to let the suspected crook know.

Seeming satisfied, the woman sat down and beckoned to someone across the lounge. Immediately a man, obviously also a foreigner, joined them and, without making an introduction, her companion spoke to him in French.

"It is all right. We can speak freely. She only understands English. I cannot get rid of her because she helped me to escape from Marshaws — and Jacques."

The man drew a quick breath and dropped his

voice to a whisper. Sally, trying to make her face a blank, listened as intently as she could, but the clatter of the lounge, with flight announcements being made every minute or so over the airport loud-speaker system, made it hard for her to catch more than an odd word now and then.

There was talk of a "package", a word which made her ears prick, and frequent references to "Jacques", whom they both seemed to fear. When it was evident that the couple were taking the 11.15 plane to Paris, Sally knew she must work fast.

Excusing herself, she hurried to the ticket office, where she was relieved to find a man on duty whom she knew from many other flights for *Evening Cry* assignments.

"Mike, I need your help. I must get the 11.15 plane to Paris," she told him.

"You'll be lucky. We are in the middle of the Christmas rush. There isn't a seat vacant. Come back in the New Year," he replied with a grin.

"This is important. I am after a scoop which might save a nice old man and a girl with polio from having a desperately unhappy Christmas. Please help me. I am sure you must have just one seat up your sleeve I could book."

He sighed, picked up some papers, and then brightened.

"There's a relief plane at 11.45, with a cancellation. How about that?"

"I'm sorry, but it must be the earlier plane. Can't you transfer someone to give me a chance?"

"I suppose so, seeing you are a V.I.P. in the newspaper world. Have you got any money? Not much? Well, we'll charge it to the *Cry* as usual. Passport? Good girl; I know you always carry it in that bulging handbag of yours. Right. You can take a seat on the 11.15. Good luck, Sally."

The man and woman she was stalking greeted her coldly as they entered the plane and she got as near to them as she could.

As the aircraft took off she rubbed her forehead dazedly, realising just what she had done. It was now December 23rd and the next morning she ought to have been taking a train for a Christmas holiday in the countryside of rural England. Instead, she was on a plane flying to France, with no luggage and not much money. No-one, apart from the booking clerk, knew where she was at that moment and yet she was coolly getting entangled with a pair of strangers she suspected to be crooks.

Had the woman made a genuine mistake in 'posting' the parcel in the sack? If so, her own trip to Paris was unnecessary and would need some explaining away at the office.

Quickly Sally dismissed the thought. Anyone who had made a mistake would have asked to see the manager of the store, but the fur-coated stranger had acted furtively, obviously terrified at the appearance of "Jacques" in the toy department.

Sally gazed down at the snowy fields below her and then at the English Channel which looked grey and cold through the clouds. What would her mother say if she knew her daughter, for whom she would be making such happy preparations, was off on another adventure so near to Christmas Eve? Still, the life of a reporter was like that, and Mrs Baxter had learned to keep calm when other mothers would be in a state of panic.

She came out of her day-dream when she heard the woman's voice say, "Can we return the compliment, mademoiselle, and offer you a lift in our taxi, when we get to Paris?"

"That depends where you are going," she answered quickly, and congratulated herself when the stranger said, "The Rue Blanc. It is near the Opéra."

"That would do splendidly. I would be glad of a lift."

Just what her own plans were she did not know, but she was determined not to lose sight of the pair. If she could see where they lived or were staying, she would be one step nearer in her investigations.

But luck was against her. Icy conditions delayed the landing and the Christmas bustle at the airport caught them in a tangle of traffic. It was then, trying to secure a taxi, that Sally made her first mistake.

Instinctively she broke into her best French as she tried to speed up the process. She clutched hold of a reluctant taxi-driver who had taken no notice of the man's signals and promised him a good tip if he would take the three of them to the Rue Blanc.

When she turned in triumph towards the others she found they were looking at her in horror.

54

"So you do speak French," said the woman furiously. "What is this? A plot to trap us?"

Things happened quickly then. The man, with a grunt, gave Sally a sharp push with his hand and sent her sprawling on to the ground. She leapt up as quickly as she could, but it was too late. The couple had entered the taxi, which was being driven rapidly away as she stood, scarlet-faced, knowing she had blundered.

The noise around her was bewildering. The relief plane had already arrived from England and the crowd wanting taxis was larger than ever. Sally realised that she must change some English money into French francs, and it was quite a time before she eventually got a taxi for herself, giving the address the couple had told her was their destination.

The man drove slowly for a Frenchman, as the roads were slippery with ice, and snow was again falling from the grey sky.

Suddenly he looked in his driving-mirror and said, "Mademoiselle, have you a friend seeking you? We are being followed, and the man inside the cab is signalling that he wants us to stop."

Sally, shivering with cold and a nameless fear, looked behind. Leaning out of the following car was the swarthy man she had last seen in the toy department earlier that morning, the mysterious Jacques who had frightened the couple who had eluded her.

His dark face looked sinister and for a moment she closed her eyes to shut out the sight.

The taximan repeated his question. "Do you want me to stop? Do you want to join your friend?" he persisted.

"No. Go faster, faster. I will pay you well if you can get away from him," she panted. "Go anywhere, round the back streets. Any place where you can shake him off."

The drive became a nightmare. Looking as though he were enjoying himself, although he was adding to her fears, the man at the wheel sent his car skidding round corners, paying no attention to gendarmes' whistles or even traffic lights when they were against him.

Relentlessly, the other taxi followed, while Sally pressed herself into a corner, hanging on to the window-strap so she would not be hurled from side to side. She had no idea where she was, for this was not the Paris of the shops and big hotels in which she usually found herself.

Eventually the gap between the two taxis widen- ed and, after a few more corners had been taken, the driver grinned at his breathless passenger.

"I think we have won. The other car went straight on at the last traffic lights. You are safe, mademoiselle. What do you want to do now?"

"I will get out," said Sally weakly, realising that she had so little money that she dare not take the taxi any farther. "Thank you for helping me."

She added a good tip to the fare he asked and, shaking a little with nerves, she went into the nearest café to order a black coffee.

The hot drink revived her and she sat quietly wondering what to do next.

Once again Fate decided for her. With a sudden sense of horror, she looked up to find the swarthy Jacques coming into the café and looking straight at her.

She rose to her feet in a frantic effort to avoid him, but the man in the waterproof grasped her wrist and forced her to sink back into the chair.

"You gave me quite a chase," he said, keeping a grip on her. "It was very foolish. You must have known I would find you. Now, where are the other two? And what have you got in that big handbag of yours?"

Sally looked round the café, which was in a poor working-class district and found no face which looked as though it would be friendly. There were only a few rough-looking men at the other tables who did not look at all interested in her plight. One or two, with a quick look at Jacques, paid their bills and disappeared.

She tilted her chin, determined not to be intimidated by the stranger.

"I have my British passport, monsieur," she said proudly. "It will show you that I am a reporter on a national newspaper which takes care of its staff. If you try to harm me it will be worse for you."

To her amazement the man loosened his grip on her wrist and looked at her less menacingly.

"Show me the passport," he demanded.

Hoping she was doing the right thing, she took

the little blue book out of her handbag and, without letting go of it, opened it at the page which showed her name and profession.

"Sally Baxter? I have heard of you," said the man slowly. "Permit me to show you my credentials."

As she stared at the piece of cardboard he offered her, a wonderful sense of relief chased away her fear.

"You are a policeman," she looked blankly. "I thought you were a crook."

"And I was convinced you were one," said the man, smiling for the first time. "Judging by the company you kept today, the mistake was understandable. What were you doing with Marcel Levier, the smuggler, and Madame Mouthier? Tell me all about it over another cup of coffee and a pastry. You look shaken, mademoiselle."

Radiantly happy, Sally told him the whole story from the moment she had found Tom and Mary Inman accused of theft to the frustration she had experienced when the two foreigners had escaped at the airport.

The French detective grasped her hand, but this time it was in a warm and friendly manner.

"Congratulations, Miss Reporter. It is no wonder your name is becoming famous. You have done a wonderful job for me as well as your newspaper. The address you gave me, the Rue Blanc, is the last link in my own investigations. I think that before the day is out your two companions will be locked up. If you will come with me I will take you to the police station, where you can rest and be warm until I have news for you."

It was evening when Sally heard the whole story after the capture of Marcel Levier and the woman in the mink coat.

Madame Mouthier, a Swiss, was new to the smuggling game and had been entrusted with the package of valuable watches to take to London from Paris. She had a rendezvous with Levier in Marshaws' store, where she was to hand over the parcel. Arriving too early, she had been looking round the toy department when she had caught sight of Jacques, who had not spotted her although he had tracked her as far as the store.

Getting into a panic, she had slipped the package into Father Christmas's sack as a way of getting rid of it, feeling she would rather run the risk of incurring the smuggler's wrath than risking arrest by the French detective.

She had returned to Marshaws the next morning, instructed to find out from Santa Claus what had become of the packet, and this time Jacques was close behind her. He had been amazed to find a teenager helping her to escape, but taking the relief plane, he had followed the threesome to Paris, with the result Sally already knew.

"What will happen to Madame Mouthier?" asked Sally anxiously. "I feel rather sorry for her. She seemed to be so frightened."

"Only a light sentence. She is just a silly woman who has got into wrong company, and this is her first offence," Jacques reassured her. "Now, Sally, I know you are anxious to get home. There is a seat for you on the night plane. This time I will drive you to the airport, very slowly and safely."

It was a sleepy but happy Sally who was at Marshaws' store early the next morning demanding to see the manager and placing before him all the typed and signed evidence needed to clear Tom and Mary Inman of the accusations brought against them.

"Can they have their jobs back today and can I be the person to tell them?" she begged.

"Certainly. Assure them we are very pleased and anxious to apologise," she was told.

Later in the day, with her suitcase in her hand, Sally snatched a minute on the way to catch her train to Nashbridge to visit the store which had provided her with such a wonderful story for the *Evening Cry*.

Across the crowded toy department she waved to Father Christmas, whose blue eyes were twinkling as merrily as ever, and caught a glimpse of Mary's radiant face as she bent to catch a whispered address from one of the children who pressed round her table.

She turned away and hurried off to the station. It would be a happy Christmas after all.

PEARL RIVER ADVENTURE

Shirley Flight leaned forward in the taxi, excitement in her blue eyes as she looked out on the teeming streets of Hong Kong.

It was an hour since she had arrived at Kai Tak Airport with a plane full of troops and their families, and now she had three days and nights of liberty — wonderful time in which to explore.

She hugged herself with delight as she looked on the traffic-choked Queen's Road, at the crimson-painted Chinese characters on the fronts of the buildings.

People surged in the middle of the road and ignored the traffic, seeming only to understand the cries of the rickshaw pullers. "'Way 'shaw! 'Way 'shaw!"

At the Oriental Hotel, Shirley paid off the taxi and stood on the pavement, her nose wrinkled as she savoured the mixed aromas of cardamon and curries, fish and incense, which was China.

Case in hand she entered the hotel lobby and stood there for a moment looking around. She was jerked into surprise as a voice at her elbow said quietly: "If I didn't know it was impossible, I'd say that you were Tracy Brandon! Same hair, same eyes, same figure."

Shirley turned to stare at the young Navy pilot a foot or so behind her, cap in hand, his blonde hair and blue eyes oddly at variance with the Orientals around them.

"Lieutenant Geoff Russell, R.N.," he saluted. "I'm sorry to scare you like that, but the resemblance to a friend of mine was so marked that I couldn't help speaking to you."

"I'm Shirley Flight, Transcontinental Airlines," she replied, beginning to move off towards the reception desk.

"Look, we can't talk here," he urged, following her. "And I want to do just that — no," he put out a hand, "I'm not trying to be impertinent, but please will you have dinner with me?"

"I'm afraid that's impossible," Shirley protested. "And I don't think that you have anything to say that could possibly interest me, Lieutenant."

She put down her bag and picked up the pen to register, but was restrained by the desperate look which came into the young officer's eyes, and her curiosity was aroused when he spoke again.

"Please, if you won't have dinner with me, will you spare me five minutes?" he pleaded.

"I shall be dining with my crew," she said, relenting a little. "And before then I have to unpack and shower, but if you'd like to join us at half-past seven you'll be welcome."

A smile lit up his sun-tanned face. "Seven-thirty it shall be," he agreed. "May I bring a friend?"

"I suppose so," she looked at him doubtfully,

anxious to escape and relax in her room for the brief time before the meal.

As she bathed and changed into a cool, silk frock, Shirley wondered about the strange behaviour of the young naval man. "Well, at least," she consoled herself, "I can hardly come to any harm with Captain Evans and the crew around. Perhaps Lieutenant Russell was suffering from too much sun. Perhaps he won't come, anyhow."

Still wondering, she ran a comb through her hair and was ready.

As she entered the foyer she saw that she had been wrong in her estimation of Geoff Russell, for he was standing there by the reception desk, immaculate in his tropical dress uniform, and with him was a tall, dark man of his own age, keen-eyed, but with a worried look creasing his forehead.

The rest of the crew were there, too, and after quick introductions went into dinner.

Clark Brandon, Geoff's friend, sat next to Shirley, but spoke very little, and it was not until coffee arrived that he seemed to relax.

"I'm amazed by your likeness to my sister," he began. "Geoff mentioned her to you, didn't he?"

"Yes." Shirley stirred her coffee thoughtfully.

"I'm a newspaper reporter on the *South China Times* and Tracy's a photographer. We work together, Miss Flight, and I'm so worried about her. She is trapped in mainland China somewhere around Macao, and has a kitful of pictures of men who were prisoners-of-war, reported dead in Korea. Those men are still alive and with those pictures as proof, the government will act to have them restored to their families. Tracy has gone into hiding in the hope that she can smuggle the films back to Hong Kong, but it's three weeks since I heard anything of her, and I'm scared."

As she listened to his story, Shirley thrilled. All about her was the sound of clacking Cantonese accent, and somewhere in the distance a weird-sounding orchestra was wailing out the old tune of "Rose, Rose, I love you".

At last Clark leaned back, it was then that Shirley realised that the rest of the party had been listening to his story.

"Macao! Now, there's an idea," Captain Evans said. "How about a trip to Pearl River? It's Portugese territory."

"Except for the island in the river, sir," Geoff put in.

"There are casinos there just like Monte Carlo," Evans went on. "Palm shaded streets, and it's a nice run on the ferry, exactly like going to the Isle of Man."

"Except for the machine-guns on the ship, and the armed guards," Clark said grimly.

"Don't be a spoil-sport," Shirley reproved. "I think it's a good idea. Could we go tomorrow?"

"We'll all go," Barry Clinton, radio operator on Shirley's flight, smiled. "Macao, here we come."

"Count me out," Clark smiled ruefully. "My

66

name is mud in Macao. I'll just stay here in Hong Kong and worry myself sick about Tracy. She's a resourceful girl, my sister, but the police in Macao are going to prove much more clever." He lowered his voice as he turned to Shirley. "I'm glad you're going though, you may be able to pick up some news about her."

"Surely the Consulate could get her back without trouble," puzzled Shirley.

"They could, but she'd have to leave the pictures behind and she won't do that unless there's no other way. She wants to help those poor men and she's pretty determined to do it."

"Bring a change of clothing with you," Russell advised as they went towards the lift and their rooms. "It gets terribly hot in Macao, and we'll get hotel rooms so that we can freshen up."

It seemed strange to Shirley to have to take a travelling bag on a day's outing, but she obeyed Russell's instructions and packed undies and a silk dress the next morning. She was wearing her uniform to travel in and when she met Barry in the hall and saw Russell coming in through the swing doors she looked around for Captain Evans.

"The boss can't come," Barry said. "He's been called over to the airport, something wrong with an engine and the maintenance men want him there. He says to be careful and not get into any trouble."

"As though we would," Shirley chuckled.

She thought about the times that warning had

been given to her, and the times she had disobeyed it. Today, she knew, there would be no opportunity to get into trouble, with the tall figures of her escorts acting like guards.

It was a four hour trip from Hong Kong to Macao and every minute of it was packed with interest for Shirley as she watched the sampans going out on their fishing trips, queer, overloaded little craft which looked so frail and yet must have been tough to judge by the amount of tackle and crews they carried.

It was overwhelmingly hot and humid, even on the water where there should have been a breeze, and the girl was glad when at last Macao came into view and the gang-plank was lowered.

This was the East all right, she thought, as she stepped from the upper deck of the vessel and wrinkled her nose at the mixture of smells which arose as she walked onto the dockside. About the quay was a crowd of rickshaw boys waiting for customers. There were hawkers with trays of oriental souvenirs which fascinated Shirley, but she was dragged away by Russell.

"They've probably been made in England," he grinned.

On their way into town, Shirley wondered why they had bothered to come to Macao. After the beauty of Hong Kong it appeared dirty and un-attractive and even the couple of modern sky-scrapers looming up ahead did nothing to convince her that she was going to enjoy this trip.

She was looking forward to the coolness of the shower and the joy of changing into a thin dress, and when they reached the Grand Hotel was grateful to be ushered to a room on the third floor. The shades were drawn, and the floor cool to her bare feet as she took off her shoes and stockings before she discarded even the forage cap of her blue-grey uniform.

A soft step behind her made her stand a minute, heart thudding before she turned, relief in her face as she saw the small figure of the Chinese girl who stood there, head bowed, hands discreetly hidden in the wide sleeves of the kimono.

"Me maid, Lee Marlin. Come to help Missy unpack. Run bath. You need wash-wash woman?"

Shirley smiled and ran a hand through her damp, fair curls.

"Thank you, Lee Marlin," she said. "But I am only here for a short visit. I do not need clothes washing. You may run a bath for me if . . ."

She drew back as the girl raised her head and stared at her, the dark, oriental eyes wide, something like fear touching the smooth face.

"Missy Brandon," the maid breathed. "How you get away? How you come here? What uniform do you wear? It is not safe, you must go quickly."

Shirley put out a hand in an attempt to soothe the servant.

"Lee Marlin, I am not Miss Brandon," she said quickly. "I am Shirley Flight, an English air hostess here to sightsee for one day."

"I not believe you." Still there was incredulity in the Chinese face. "You Missy Brandon. I know you. You live here for long time. I know you go into hiding after police see you."

"Look." Shirley fished desperately in her zip bag and brought out her passport. "This will show you who I am. Look, picture of me, Shirley Flight. Can you read that?"

It took a full ten minutes to convince the girl that she was mistaken and another ten to assure her that the uniform was not a disguise, and by that time Shirley was becoming more and more interested in the mysterious Tracy Brandon. She was also becoming dimly aware of Geoff Russell's reason for getting to know her. He had booked the rooms at this hotel and must have known that the floor maid would think that her former mistress had come back.

"Lee," she began, when the girl returned from the bathroom where she had been laying out fresh towels. "Where is Tracy Brandon?"

The Chinese girl gave her an inscrutable glance and shrugged. "I not know," she said briefly.

"Yes, I think you do." Shirley faced her. "I would like to help her and I cannot do that if you won't do your share."

"You speak true?"

"Yes, I do."

Funnily enough, Shirley thought as she watched the other girl's face, *I do want to help. My life seems to have become entangled with this stranger's. I know what it's like to be in trouble after all my adventures, and if I can help Tracy then I'm going to.*

Aloud, she said, "Lee, you must tell me where Miss Brandon is so that I can go and talk to her."

The maid studied Shirley carefully for a minute, and then she smiled gravely. "I trust you, Missy Flight. Now Missy Brandon is hiding in far part of town in hotel where my sister works. I told her to go there."

Shirley walked over to the window and looked down on the crowded street. "Will you take me to this place?"

The girl shook her head. "That I dare not do. I tell you name. You go alone. The police they have already spoken to me and they watch me."

"Very well." Shirley bustled around the room, picking up her discarded shoes, hurrying into her stockings with scant regard for ladders. "You give me the address, and . . ." Hurriedly she found her pen and a piece of hotel notepaper. "You see that this note is delivered to Mr Clinton in room twenty-four, if I am not back before dinner to-night. You understand?"

Lee Marlin nodded. "Yes, Missy. I do that." She hesitated a moment, then added, "ask first for Su Marlin, my sister, at the Chu-Ling Hotel, Monthana."

Quickly Shirley wrote the note for Barry, wondering how best to word it, wondering what the men would say when they knew that she had taken off into the teeming streets of this strange town.

"*Barry*," she wrote, "*I have a lead on Tracy Brandon, and I am going to see her. If I'm not back in time to sail, ask the maid on my floor, Lee Marlin. She will tell you where I am.*"

"I think it better for you to stay here, Missy," there was fear in the maid's eyes as she took the envelope from Shirley. "It will need a clever person to help Miss Tracy."

"Don't worry about me." Shirley patted her arm. "I can take care of myself."

But she wondered about that as she hurried out of the hotel hallway, praying that she wouldn't see Barry or Geoff. It was one thing to be able to take care of yourself in reasonable surroundings, but Macao, she knew, wasn't that kind of a place.

She hailed a rickshaw, and as the panting boy pulled it down the main street and quickly away from the brightest lights, Shirley knew a moment of fear.

What was she letting herself in for now? She watched the rickshaw boy forcing his way through the milling crowd of people who disregarded all traffic and wandered aimlessly in the middle of the road.

The streets were growing narrower as they went, and now there were few lights except those in tiny shops, open to the street; where sinister looking Chinese waited by their wares — strange looking foodstuffs, bright cheap clothing and shiny souvenirs all laid out in profusion.

The Chu-Ling Hotel lay in the narrowest street of all, where overhanging buildings, ancient and dirty, almost touched overhead. There was no air and very little light. Shirley shuddered as the boy pulled up before the dingy front of the place.

It was half-an-hour since they had left the Grand Hotel, but to Shirley it felt like a lifetime. She roused herself to pay the boy, and felt as though she were losing a friend as he pattered off down the street.

The hall of the little hotel was brighter than the outside, for it was hung with quaint banners bearing Chinese signs, and the young girl who came forward to greet Shirley was pretty in her flowery native dress.

"I am looking for Su Marlin," Shirley began. "Her sister, Lee, sent me here."

"I am Su." The girl bowed her head, but not before Shirley had seen the quick interest her uniform had brought.

"My sister, I trust she is well?"

"Quite well. Su, I wish to talk to Miss Brandon. Will you take me to her at once? It is urgent. I have little time."

For an instant she thought that Su was going to refuse, but then the solemn brown eyes, meeting hers, reassured her. "You follow me, Missy, please?"

Tracy Brandon's room was at the very top of the hotel, up steep stairs, down uneven corridors then behind two locked doors.

When the second door was opened and Shirley was face to face with the photographer, she gazed at the girl who came forward, amazed.

It was like looking into a mirror, she thought dazedly as she took in the blue eyes, the short, fair hair only a shade darker than her own. Tracy was of the same height, a little fatter, but the resemblance was so marked that Su, who had not shown any wonder in the beginning, now stared from one to the other, her eyes wide.

Quickly Shirley explained who she was, and her reason for being there, and Tracy, recovered from the shock of seeing her double, pushed a chair forward.

"I'll be glad of a new brain," she said grimly. "I just can't think any more. After three weeks of worry I was considering giving myself up to the Consul and letting him get me away."

"What about your pictures?"

"Oh, them," Tracy shrugged. "I tried to do the impossible and hoped it would come off. But the police heard about it and are too interested in me to ever let me get away with the photos I took. I was too nosey, I reckon. Will you go back, Miss Flight, and tell my brother that I'm tired of this and will do anything to be free again?"

"No, I'm not going to do that," Shirley whipped off her cap and handed it to the girl. "There's a better way. Try that on for size."

Dubiously Tracy did as she was bidden, then stared at herself in the cracked mirror.

"It'll work," Shirley insisted. "Change clothes with me. Walk out of here as easily as I walked in. Use my passport if you have to and get back to Hong Kong. Take your pictures with you."

"Hey . . . wait a minute." Tracy crossed to where Shirley sat. "You can't mean this. You don't know what you're offering to do. It's wonderful of you, but I can't let you do it. You'll be left here. If the police come they'll question you."

"You've hidden here for three weeks," Shirley argued. "Why should they come now? I'll get away tomorrow, somehow."

"Tomorrow?" Tracy laughed. "Shirley, you're in the Far East now where there can be complications such as you've never dreamt of."

"I don't care," Shirley was stubborn; certain that this was the only way to get Tracy and the films to safety. "Hurry, change clothes with me."

Still the other girl hesitated. "I don't like to get you involved in any trouble," she insisted. "You're very kind and I appreciate it."

"Then get into this." Whilst Tracy had been talking, Shirley had taken off her uniform coat and skirt and was unbuttoning her blouse. "And don't worry about me. I'm perfectly innocent and I'll get away. The important thing is that you must get those pictures back and help those men."

"Missy right," Su put in, holding out Shirley's blouse. "You go."

"When you reach the Grand Hotel," Shirley said as she slipped Tracy's cotton dress over her head, "go straight to room thirty-six. Geoff Russell and my radio operator are in twenty-four. Lee Marlin will contact them. And do hurry because if one of us isn't back by dinner-time they'll all be in a panic. Have you got the films?"

"Yes," Tracy held out a small packet.

"Slip them into the inside lining of the cap," Shirley advised. "My passport is in the pocket of the jacket."

"You know what trouble you'll be in for if this doesn't work, don't you?" Tracy's voice was grim.

"I know. And let me worry about it." Shirley gave her a little push. "Now, go, and good luck."

"You're a wonderful person, Shirley Flight." Tracy, leaning forward, gave the other girl a quick hug and a kiss. "Thank you."

"I'll see you in Hong Kong," Shirley called with a lightness she was far from feeling as she watched the others leave the little room, and heard the key turn in the lock.

Her heart sank as she looked out of the window and saw the Chinese policeman patrolling up and down the narrow street. Had he seen her come into the hotel? Was he waiting to find out what an English air hostess might be doing in this squalid part of town?

She watched breathlessly until the figure of Tracy Brandon, neat and upright in the borrowed uniform, appeared and walked briskly away from the Chu-Ling Hotel to stand on the corner of the street and casually hail a rickshaw.

The policeman stopped and stared for a minute but made no move toward the rickshaw and its occupant. Shirley turned away from the window and sank into a chair, aware that her legs were trembling and her heart thudding with the anxiety of the past few minutes.

There was little to do in the small room except to glance through the books which Tracy had left, and within an hour Shirley was suffering from a bad attack of nerves.

What a fool she had been to hand her passport over to a strange girl. A girl who, through striking resemblance, could take the passport and use it as she wished. Perhaps she would not even go near the Grand Hotel, but take off on some other mad photographic adventure.

Cold shivers ran down Shirley's back and she wanted to scream. Why had she been so impetuous? What on earth was Captain Evans going to say when he heard of this escapade? That he would be angry was putting it mildly.

She began to pace the room, remembering the peculiar circumstances of her meeting with Lieutenant Russell. The whole affair had been a frame-up and she had been silly enough to fall for it.

Doubts and fears chased madly through her brain until, just before dusk, the shy Su Marlin unlocked the door and came softly into the room, carrying a tray.

In spite of her terror, Shirley's mouth watered as

she saw the delicious food which the girl laid out on the table. There were all kinds of tempting Chinese dishes and when at last Su poured out the clear China tea into the handleless cup and handed it to her, Shirley began to feel brighter.

By now, if everything was as Tracy and her brother had said, the other girl must be back at the Grand Hotel and within the next hour on her way back across the ferry to Hong Kong.

She knew that Barry Clinton would hate to go without her and would be working on some kind of scheme to get her back to safety, but she could not think how he would be able to do it without arousing the suspicions of Captain Evans.

It was a struggle to lie down on the hard bed and try to sleep that night, for so many things were harassing Shirley and not the least of them was the fact that by her foolish action it might be a very long time before she saw either England or any of her friends.

"You're a fool," she told herself sternly at last. "You brought it all on yourself, and you know what a good friend Barry is. He'll do something."

She was up early, glad of the chance to stretch her legs and ease her back after the sleepless night on the unrelenting bed. When Su came in with breakfast Shirley saw that the Chinese girl had brought English newspapers. At least they would help to pass the time, but before lunchtime she had read them from cover to cover, including the adverts.

The rest of that day was endless, only broken by the smiling Su when she brought food, and because of her duties in the hotel the girl could not stay to chat.

It was early evening when Shirley, dreading the thought of another night in the confined little room, heard the sound of footsteps and the key once again turning in the lock.

The footsteps were purposeful and ominous and the soft little shuffle of Su's native slippers accompanied them.

It was a scared little Chinese girl who appeared first in the doorway, eyes wide, mouth tremulous. "I bring visitor," she announced fearfully.

Shirley's heart felt as though it were turning over. This was it, then. The police had found Tracy's hiding place at last. She searched her brain feverishly for words to convince the official that she was not Tracy Brandon, and realised at the same time that she had no proof. That all she had to identify herself was the other girl's passport!

Looking up fearfully she met the piercing gaze of — Captain Evans!

Her first feeling was of thankfulness that Tracy had got to safety and that after all her story had been true, but she quailed as she saw the look in the Captain's eyes.

He was carrying a small zipped bag which he handed to her with a curt, "get into these and look slippy," and the look on his face did not soften.

As he turned towards the door he looked back

and shook his head slowly from side to side making a despairing, "Tck! Tck! Tck!"

Shirley straightened her shoulders, trying hard to appear her usual efficient self in spite of the rumpled frock and her tousled fair hair.

"I'll wait outside," he said briefly, and was gone.

Eagerly she explored the contents of her bag. There was her uniform, neatly folded, and in the pocket her passport.

It was a matter of five minutes to change and stuff Tracy's dress into the bag, then to open the door and say in a small voice, "I'm ready, sir."

Evans kept up the silence all the way down the narrow stairs to where Su waited in the hall. "Good luck, Missy," she smiled, showing her even teeth.

"Thank you," Shirley managed to smile back, and then she was following the Captain out into the street.

What had previously been a quiet side street was transformed now, Shirley saw with sinking heart. An army lorry, pulling up at the opposite end, disgorged half-a-dozen soldiers. There was more than one policeman, too, and she swallowed hard as she realised it would only have been a matter of minutes before the men would have been clattering up the stairs of the Chu-Ling Hotel. For it was obvious that the authorities had heard of Tracy Brandon's hideout and were coming to search for her; and for the pictures which they wanted to stop being published.

"Keep your head high and walk quickly," breathed Captain Evans grimly. "If there's any talking to be done leave it to me. I can't think why I should help you but . . ."

He quickened his pace as he spoke, and Shirley found it hard to keep up with him in her high-heeled court shoes. If she hadn't known him so well, she would have sworn that he was enjoying this adventure — maybe, she thought, she didn't know him so well after all.

They passed the army truck and Shirley's heart thudded wildly as the sergeant in charge of the men eyed the English pair curiously. He advanced a step as though to challenge them, but stepped aside when the Captain charged on. Two minutes more, and around the next corner, a car awaited them, and without ceremony Evans thrust Shirley into it. At once the driver let in the clutch and set off at breakneck speed down the narrow streets to pull up with a screech in front of the Grand Hotel.

Still Captain Evans was silent and grim as he hailed another cab and ordered the driver to make for the ferry. "We've ten minutes to catch the night boat," he said, "and if we don't make it, we've had it. Those army men will be on our tails once they've searched that hotel."

All the questions which rose to Shirley's lips were silenced by anxiety as she watched the road behind them, keeping her fingers crossed when the driver was held up, first by traffic and then by the inevitable lazy road crossers.

But at last the quay came into view and she found herself hustled into Customs. Luckily there were few passengers and they reached the deck of the ferry, the last to board as the crew hauled in the gangplank.

She took a deep breath and leaned against the rail watching the dock grow further away as the vessel chugged out into the river.

"There you are," Captain Evans, fanning his face with his uniform cap, pointed to where the army truck crashed to a stop within inches of the edge of the dock, and the men piled out to stand, staring up at the now quickly moving ship. "It was a close thing, and you're the silliest girl I ever knew . . ."

"Please sir," Shirley was determined to ask one question before she settled down to the lecture which she knew was coming and which she deserved. "Is Tracy Brandon all right?"

"Thanks to you, yes. She came back to Hong Kong with Clinton and Russell. Barry wanted to come back for you, but I thought it was my duty to do that. I'm not very good at intrigue, Miss Flight, and the only way I could think of to get you out was the obvious one, in your own clothes."

"Thank you sir," Shirley said gratefully, and was about to apologise further, but was stopped by his hand on her arm.

"You look all in," he said gruffly. "Let's go down for a meal and some coffee. I could use them and I'm sure you could, too. We shall say no more about this little trip, seeing that it's turned out all right after all. But remember, I'm getting too old for rescue work, so next time you're on my flight behave yourself. And that's an order."

"Yes, sir," Shirley smiled up at him, her blue eyes twinkling.

Captain Evans, she thought, was a very understanding man after all.

THE LANDSLIDE

Julie Ross, the youngest travel courier employed by "GO", relaxed in the front seat of the coach as it left Lake Como speeding on towards Locarno in Switzerland. Her passengers were settled after a good breakfast and a wonderful five days in Italy, and Julie eased off her shoes, knowing that from now until they reached their mid-morning stop she could enjoy the scenery.

Now, after one season's work for the firm, the small, dark girl, with the freckled nose and the friendly brown eyes, was more confident, and the party she was in charge of made her more so. For they were all kind people with not a moaner amongst them.

Her driver, Angus Finlay, a young stocky Scot with the reddest hair she had ever seen, was a tower of strength, often going out of his way to help her.

The road ahead unwound upwards like a ribbon, the heat haze already shimmering so that it seemed the coach would soon run into a lake. All around were mountains covered by pine trees and broken only by an occasional house, its windows shining as the morning sun caught them.

Coffee and cream cakes in Bellinzona broke the morning run, and now the route was breathtaking, the mountainous road so narrow that it would be impossible for two coaches to pass. Way down below, many hundreds of feet to the right, was a sheer drop and one or two of the more timid passengers shuddered as they looked down.

Angus, handling the big coach expertly, was singing happily as they rounded yet another hairpin bend, but his song stopped abruptly, and Julie peered up ahead to see what had caused him to slow down.

She gasped as she saw, only a few feet in front of them, the great pile of rocks and boulders which completely blocked the road.

"A wee landslide," Angus whistled through his teeth.

"Now what do we do?" Julie opened the door to climb down on to the road, the passengers following, to stand and stare too.

"We'll have to go back." Angus shrugged. "Take a day to shift that lot. Yes, we'll have to go back and tell the local police."

"But we can't turn," Julie protested.

"Not here," he admitted cheerfully. "We'll have to go backwards until we come to the lay-by."

Julie shivered. "My people aren't going to like that," she said, aware that there was nothing else for it but to try.

Unwilling to accept the driver's decision, she walked over to the boulders and climbed over some of them. It was then that she saw, half buried by the rocks, a car, its bonnet crushed, windscreen shattered. Her eyes grew wide when, moving a little closer, she thought she saw a movement. She looked again, afraid of what she might see.

Something moved again! That made Julie leap into action and she scrambled back to where Angus stood looking down the steep road.

"Angus! There's a car under those rocks and I think there's someone in it," she whispered urgently.

He stared at her. "There can't be anyone alive under that lot."

"Please come and look," she begged.

He followed her down the other side of the landslide where the condition of the car was clearer. There he bent down, pulling at one of the rear doors, struggling to get it open.

They both saw the man who was spread-eagled half-way over the front seat, as though he had seen the beginning of the fall and tried to get away from it.

"I don't think he's badly hurt." Angus wormed his way into the wreck and looked at the unconscious man.

"What can we do?" Julie held the door wide so that the driver could examine the man. "We shouldn't move him, it says in all the first-aid books. . . ."

Angus came up for air and grinned at her. "This is a time we must forget the books, my bonnie," he said briskly. "We've got to get him out of here and bandage that cut on his head. Then we've got to turn the coach around and get him back to a hospital. Don't talk," he added as he saw her mouth open. "Just help me."

Somehow they got the man out. He was small and slim and Angus was strong, so that all Julie had to do was to guide him back to the road. At last they laid the stranger carefully on the narrow grass verge.

"I'll go for my case," Julie suggested. "I've got some first-aid kit. . . ."

The words had scarcely left her mouth when the loud sound of a motor horn made them look up at the next bend in the road.

"Quick!" Angus stood up. "We've got to stop this fellow from coming round that bend and bashing into the rocks."

Julie was the quicker off the mark, and she ran, stumbling in her high-heeled shoes, towards the oncoming vehicle, whipping out her hankie and waving it at the long, continental coach which rushed towards her. Brakes screeched then, and the driver jumped down.

Quickly the girl explained what had happened, noting as she talked that the coach was empty and that it belonged to the same firm as their own.

"I was just on my way with a relief coach," the driver said.

"I know!" Julie had a sudden inspiration. "You could take *our* coach, and my passengers could climb over the rocks into yours. That would save time and neither of us would be off schedule."

"Clever girl," he agreed.

"Not so clever," she smiled. "Just terrified of going backwards down that dreadful road."

It took twenty minutes to turn the coaches and transfer the passengers and their luggage. Then the two drivers carried the unconscious man and settled him on the back seat, with Julie sitting on the floor beside him, praying that they had not made him worse by moving him.

Just as the coach moved off towards Locarno, Julie's eyes were suddenly struck by a bright light which flashed across her face. She stood up quickly, looking back down the road through the rear window, and as she did so she caught the light again.

There was someone up on the side of the hill which fringed the road. Someone with a powerful pair of binoculars! But who? And why? And had they any connection with the landslide?

Who, wondered Julie, was this man who lay so still with the blood already seeping through the bandage on his head? She decided to try to find out, but felt like a spy as she unfastened the brief-case which they had found in the car.

There were some closely typed papers which she did not look at but replaced carefully. Then she found the passport which was different from any she had seen and bore the name of ROBERT ELLIS, DEPARTMENT OF INLAND REVENUE, CUSTOMS AND EXCISE.

The words leapt up at her and Julie Ross knew that she had once again stumbled into a mystery. Someone had wished this man harm and had started the landslide just when his car was passing one spot in the road. There must be a gang, she decided excitedly, for no one person could have caused all that rock to fall.

"One of these days," she admonished herself, "your imagination will land you into real trouble. You're day-dreaming again."

They were within a few minutes of their destination when Robert Ellis moved, and Julie put out a hand to steady him on the narrow seat.

"Where . . . am . . . I?" He opened his eyes and stared at her. "Who . . . are . . . you?"

She smiled at him quietly. "You had an accident. We are taking you to Locarno to a doctor."

He struggled to sit up. "I don't want to go to Locarno," he gasped. "I just left there. I've got to catch three men driving a white Land Rover. . . ."

"I'm sorry." Julie restrained him. "Your head is hurt, and your car smashed by a landslide. Do you remember that?"

He sighed. "I remember. I followed that car. Did you meet it on the road? Did you?"

"No, we met nothing all the way from Como. Look, you must have a doctor and treatment."

"Those men are desperate. I'm a customs investigator, and I've followed them for weeks."

The coach pulled up then at their hotel in Locarno, The Albergo Ticino, and before the passengers were settled, Julie and Angus helped the injured man into a bedroom immediately provided by the manager. A doctor was sent for and, whilst Julie waited for him, Angus coped with luggage and shepherded the passengers into the dining-room.

In no time at all Mr Ellis was expertly bandaged and given pills to ease his pain.

At last he was comfortable, and Julie spoke comfortingly to him. "Mr Ellis, why don't we send for the police and let them find this gang of men?"

"No. It's my job and I'll finish it. The men I followed are part of a syndicate of smugglers taking diamonds from South Africa to Europe. I want their leader."

"Well, another few hours won't matter," Julie soothed, and with that he had to be content.

After a quick lunch she went back and found him sleeping, so she went up to her room and changed into a cool cotton frock and sandals.

Now, she thought, she was prepared for anything. She would have a shot at helping the customs man. Chasing dangerous smugglers was hardly her idea of fun, but she felt so sorry for Mr Ellis, and she had two free days.

Walking out into the busy street, Julie wondered about her next move. How on earth was she to find the whereabouts of a white Land Rover? Then she remembered that there would be dozens of coach-drivers here with their parties and she knew from experience that they congregated at a little café tucked away in a side street.

As she made her way to the Apollo she was glad

to be free and out of uniform. It was hot and sunny and she felt almost like a holidaymaker as she strolled along, stopping once to admire exquisite Swiss pottery figures in the windows of a very modern shop.

She found five drivers whom she knew, but all of them shook their heads when she asked them about the car. Disappointed, she sat down at the only available table over by the service door, and ordered tea and cakes. She may as well wait and see if anyone else came in. "Don't be impatient," she told herself, "you may not even be lucky enough to find one clue. Two days isn't very long, and Mr Ellis told you he was dealing with clever and ruthless smugglers."

Idly glancing around, she saw the tall, elegantly dressed woman come in and be conducted with ceremony to a table obviously reserved for her. Julie stared enviously at the expensive, immaculate white dress, the dark hair styled in the newest fashion, but most of all she was attracted by the woman's steel-grey eyes which seemed to see everything at once, penetrating and commanding.

Julie beckoned to the waitress. "May I have some more hot water, please?" Then she added idly, "Does that woman in white live here? She is very beautiful."

The girl smiled. "She owns the pottery shop and has a studio where she designs. Her name is Selma Kroll."

Julie remembered the shop where she had

stopped, and then her attention was taken by the appearance of a slim young man dressed in local costume. He carried a guitar and, circling the tables, began to sing. Julie watched him absently, and then keenly as he drew level with Miss Kroll's table. Was it her imagination or did a sharp glance pass from those grey eyes to the brown ones? Hadn't his hand stopped strumming long enough to meet briefly the scarlet-tipped one of the woman?

Then, as he finally slipped out of the service door after his act, and stood there acknowledging the applause, Julie's heart began to thud wildly.

For she could clearly see through the wide window beyond the door, the white Land Rover parked at the back of the café!

She called for her bill and thought about her next move impatiently as the waitress seemed deliberately slow. She must get back to the hotel and tell Mr Ellis what she had seen. Then he would certainly have to let the police handle the case, for he wasn't fit to do it.

Julie ran back down the streets, bumping into people, almost being knocked down by cars. At the hotel, without waiting to knock, she rushed into Mr Ellis's room, and then stood, eyes wide with astonishment, as she saw the empty bed, clothes flung back as though the man had left in a hurry.

"Oh, heavens," she said aloud. "Perhaps he's worse and they've taken him to hospital."

Fuming at the waste of time, she made her way

to the office, but the manager was as suprised as she was.

"He hasn't left here, I'm certain," he assured her, going to the empty room to stare about him perplexed. "I came up to see him an hour ago. We shall have to call the police. . . ."

"No, please," Julie put a hand on his arm. "Not just yet. I think I may be able to find him. Don't ask any questions but give me a few hours."

"Well," he looked doubtful. "It's most irregular, but . . . I'll do as you ask. I hope you know what you're doing."

So do I, thought Julie ruefully. Oh, so do I.

She wandered disconsolately out on to the veranda, her mind a muddle of plans which she discarded as soon as she thought of them.

When she saw Angus walking towards her she could have hugged him. Here was someone she could talk to. Perhaps he would be able to help.

He listened to her story with the hint of a grin on his sunburned face, but he had grown serious by the time she was finished.

"Let's go back to the café," he suggested. "That's the best thing to do. We can plan as we go."

Waiting to cross the busy road, Julie's attention was taken by the shabby old man who stood by the doorway of a shop directly opposite to the hotel. He looked so inconspicuous, but somehow had an air of mystery about him. He *seemed* disinterested in the passers-by, but yet he glanced up quickly each time anyone left the building.

"Come on, lassie, stop your day-dreaming or we'll never get across," Angus's broad accent brought her back to her senses, and she allowed him to lead her into the maze of traffic and to safety on the other side of the road.

"Let's take a wee walk around the block," he suggested when at last they reached the Apollo. "Then we can see if the car's still there."

She agreed eagerly, but they were both abashed when they saw the high wall which surrounded the rear of the place.

"There's a gate," Julie said tentatively. "If we could open it just a crack. . . ."

"Someone'll see us and think we're going to rob the café." Angus sounded dour.

"Oh, all right, if you're scared. . . ." Julie marched up to the gate and tried the heavy latch. It gave way and she found herself peering intently through the three-inch opening.

Angus stood behind her, breathing heavily down her neck, and in spite of herself she gave a low chuckle. "Stop breathing," she whispered. "It tickles!"

They both saw the Land Rover then, and in a startled instant heard its engine roar into life. Julie felt as if she were rooted to the spot. For the man in the driving-seat was the guitar singer!

Just in time, Angus wrenched the gate shut and tugged at her arm. They ran back down the alleyway to stand panting outside the café.

"We've got to follow him," the girl said urgently.

"On our own four feet?" Angus was scornful. "Wait. I know a chap at the garage around the corner. I'll nip there and borrow a car. It'll take a minute or two for that fellow to open the gate. You watch his direction."

"Do hurry." Julie watched him go.

It was ten minutes before the Land Rover came out, turning on to the road which led out of Locarno, and Julie wondered what had happened to Angus.

Fifteen minutes, twenty. It was too late now. Furious at the delay, Julie walked towards the street where Angus had gone. There was no sign of him.

She stared back at the café and there, sitting at a window table, was the old man who had been standing across from the hotel. Who was he, and what did he want? She wondered about him vaguely, worried about the disappearance of Angus.

It was late afternoon when she finally admitted to herself that the coach-driver was not coming back and she made her way back to the hotel, hopefully.

She was relieved to find that the manager was off duty so at least she wouldn't have to answer any awkward questions about Mr Ellis, who still had not returned to his room.

Julie changed for dinner feeling as though the sight of food would choke her. But she managed to eat a little and was cheered by the appearance of

one of her fellow "GO" couriers who breezed into the dining-room for a quick meal before taking her party on to a show.

"Saw old Angus half an hour ago," the girl said.

"Where did you see him?" Julie demanded.

"In a smashing car with a beautiful brunette. They were driving up the road towards Appensea — you know, the deserted village. Hey, where are you going?"

Julie sat down as quickly as she had stood up. "Nowhere," she said dully. But what, she wondered, had made Angus desert her and go off with Selma Kroll, for it was obvious that she was his companion.

Neither of the men had returned when Julie went reluctantly to bed. There seemed to be nothing else to do. At midnight she was still awake, and in desperation she got up and dressed. Slipping a light woolly over her thin dress she went outside. Again the old man was over by the shop and the girl had a wild idea that he might be watching her. Hurrying down the road towards the lake, she stood at last looking out over the water, the reflection of the mountains and the twinkling lights.

It was then that she heard a car stop on the narrow roadway and the soft voice of a woman. "Miss Ross, I believe?"

Julie turned and saw Selma Kroll. In the back seat was the man who had played the guitar at the café.

"Your friend Angus has had an accident. He would like to see you."

"See me?" Julie was poised for flight, but she was too late. Strong hands were on her arms and before she could utter a sound she was pushed into the car.

"Let me go! Let me go!"

The couple took no notice and Miss Kroll drove the car swiftly up the narrow road and into the village, which Julie recognised as Appensea, for she had brought many of her tourists up here.

The car stopped before an old, deserted house and Julie was bundled out, up steep stairs and pushed into a moonlit room.

"Angus!" She ran to the figure over by the window.

Quickly he told her how he had been taken away in the car by a man who flourished a revolver. How Miss Kroll had brought him here.

"Listen," he ended. "There's a plane coming tonight to pick this gang up. Miss Kroll is the boss. The guitar singer and the pilot of the plane have been doing the smuggling for her. We got too interested, that's why they captured us."

"We've got to get away," Julie determined. "But how? Oh, Angus, that's a plane circling now."

Suddenly she clutched his arm. "Below this window there's a parapet and below that a flat roof. Could we . . .?"

He grinned. "I reckon I could. What's a broken neck between friends? But it'll mean breaking the window and that's going to make a terrific noise."

Julie whipped off her cardigan and smiled. "Take off a shoe to break the glass, and blanket the sound with my woolly," she said urgently. "We can't waste any time."

Her heart felt as though it would burst as she waited for Angus to do the work which could mean freedom. It would be awful if their captors came along now and stopped them.

But at least the sound was dulled by the thickness of the cardigan and in a matter of minutes they were out on the narrow ledge. It was a good thing that it was dark, Julie thought as she tried to avoid looking down. At least it hid the dreadful drop to the hard ground.

Cautiously she followed the driver along the ledge. There was no sound from their captors and the girl kept her fingers crossed as she edged forward.

"I'm going to jump now," whispered Angus. "When I say go, you follow me."

Dazedly she obeyed. How on earth were they going to stop the criminals now that they were free? They had no way of getting into town, and she realised for the first time what a hopeless task they had set themselves.

It seemed an age before they were on the ground, standing for a moment to peer helplessly about them. Then Julie snapped her fingers excitedly.

"Angus, I've got it," she said. "I know how we can delay that plane. Then you can go for help whilst I wait here. Come on."

"Just a minute," he panted after her.

"I haven't got one to spare." Julie rushed on, taking advantage of the cover of the trees towards the field where they could see the outline of the plane.

"We're going to let the air out of those tyres," she flung the words back over her shoulder.

They were stumbling on over rough stones and somehow over the wall into the field. Then the aircraft loomed above them and they began their task. A loud hiss came from Angus's side as the tyre deflated and Julie struggled on to release the valve on her side.

But even as she accomplished the job they both heard footsteps on the cobbled road.

"They're coming. We've got to hide." Angus was anxious.

"You go." Julie gave him a push. "Bring anyone you can find." She ran for the shelter of the trees.

The two men and Miss Kroll came into view almost at once, each carrying a small case, and the girl watched as they climbed into the plane. She heard the engine turn into life and saw the dim outline of the propellers as they began to turn.

With bated breath she waited for the pilot to find why the craft wouldn't taxi, but it was five minutes before the engine stopped again and the passengers climbed out to inspect the machine.

They walked round with flashlights and she heard their exclamations as they located the trouble.

"We should have *punctured* the tyres," she realised suddenly. "Then they couldn't have mended them quickly. As it is they can pump them up or something."

Julie was so deep in thought that the brilliant light of a flashlight glancing about the field, catching her hideout, blinded her and made her aware that she had been discovered. Too late she tried to run farther, out of that searching beam of light.

It was then that everything seemed to happen at once.

The field, a second ago so silent, seemed to be full of uniformed men, dark forms all advancing on the aeroplane and the three people who stood transfixed by it. Julie heard Angus's voice calling to her and she moved towards the sound, thankful that he had found help in time.

But the first person she recognised as she ran towards the leading party was the old man who had been so mysteriously following her.

Now she knew him and ran to him, laughing and crying with relief. He was Mr Ellis!

It was almost daylight when the three of them finally sat down to a late meal in the deserted dining-room of their hotel.

Julie, so tired that she could hardly keep her eyes open was excited by the capture of the smugglers, and Mr Ellis, now changed into his own

clothing, a small plaster over the cut on his head, was triumphant.

"My department will never be able to thank you enough for what you have done today, Miss Ross," he smiled.

Julie blushed. "If you hadn't come along with the police . . ." she began.

"It was a good thing you weren't depending on me," said Angus. "Meeting Mr Ellis and the others was a stroke of luck. I couldn't see anyone around *to* help."

"One thing I would like to know, if it isn't a great secret," Julie went on, "is how it all started."

The customs man stirred his coffee thoughtfully. "It began many months ago," he began. "We knew that diamonds were being smuggled out of South Africa and into Switzerland and Italy but we couldn't find the method until one day in the customs shed. . . ."

Julie leaned forward, fully awake now. "Go on," she prompted.

"One of our men, examining a passenger's luggage took from it a porcelain figure and dropped it. It was Swiss and was of William Tell shooting the apple from his son's head. That apple contained a diamond. Well, we arrested the man who was carrying it, but he wouldn't give away any of his associates."

Julie gasped and Angus whistled softly.

"The figures, we have now found, were made by Miss Kroll and smuggled out by her agents. She

108

made one big mistake and that was to keep the models all alike. We confiscated several, but not all of them held diamonds. She never sold this model in her shop so we could not pin our suspicions on to her. But now, thanks to you, we know."

He pushed his empty cup towards Julie and, like someone in a dream, she picked up the coffee-pot and replenished the cup.

"I had to get out of the hotel and adopt my disguise because I knew the gang must know of your inquisitiveness, and I had to let them go to the limit in order to catch them. But even I was worried when I saw them take you off in that car. I was scared that something dreadful would happen to you."

"It almost did on that parapet," Julie chuckled. "I hate heights."

"You're a brave girl." Mr Ellis patted her arm. "But even heroines must sleep and you're off to bed this instant or we'll have to carry you there."

"I won't sleep." She stood up stiffly. "But I've got a conducted tour to do tomorrow, so I suppose I'd better make an effort."

"You had that." Angus took her arm gently. "And mind you keep out of trouble for a while now."

"I'll try my best," Julie promised, but she knew that when the next adventure came along she would be ready!

MYSTERY ON CANVAS

Mallery Cane and Lucille Fair lugged their suitcases and painting kit down off the rack, and waited until the train stopped in Chilbury Station. Then they climbed down on to the platform of the little country station and breathed in the fragrant country air.

Mallery sniffed delightedly. "Oh, how wonderful it is," she cried. "It looks like spring here, and it smells like spring."

She then turned to lead the way out of the station and into the little forecourt, where a collection of farm transport was parked. An antique country bus stood in one corner, and an even more antique taxi-cab stood at the pavement edge waiting to pick up fares.

The two girls hailed the taxi and loaded their belongings into the back, while a couple of leisurely porters heaved their trunks on to the luggage rack at the back and roped them on.

After a casual and cheerful chat about the weather and the prospects of a wonderful summer, the girls climbed aboard, and a minute later the taxi was roaring up the narrow high street of Chilbury and up the winding hill to Chilbury Castle.

The castle had recently been converted into a school of art, and was already proving to be a great success.

110

When Mallery and Lucille had reached school-leaving age, they had persuaded their parents to allow them to enrol at the Chilbury Castle Art School for two or three years and to receive expert coaching from the proprietor, Monsieur Carrilon, the famous artist and critic who was running the establishment.

The taxi eventually reached the top of the hill and crawled round the massive walls of the castle, and over the drawbridge, and so into the grounds.

Monsieur Carrilon was waiting in the ancient stone carved doorway beneath a coloured stone crest and he smiled a cheerful welcome, while the hall porter and the taxi-driver took the girls' belongings up the wonderful oak staircase to the room that the girls were to share during their life at the school.

Mallery and Lucille were escorted to their room by the proprietor, and they cried out in delight when they entered the delightful room that had been allotted to them. The walls were oak-panelled, the floor was as smooth and mellow as honey, and the curtains and chair-covers were gay with brightly flowered chintz. The linen fold oak furniture perfected the tastefully decorated room.

"Lunch will be served in just fifteen minutes," Monsieur Carrilon informed them. "It will be in the Tudor dining-room. There you will meet your fellow-students."

After a delicious lunch of cold roast ham and fresh salad, followed by caramel custards and fruit tarts and fragrant coffee, Monsieur Carrilon rose to his feet and made a little speech of welcome. He ended by saying: "On this first afternoon of the new term, we shall all spend the time together in the famous art gallery, and I shall explain special points about some of the paintings to you and answer any questions that you may care to ask. Afterwards you will be invited to wander about at will to study and examine the paintings, or make sketches of anything that takes your fancy. Your studies will be based on your own 'bents' and individual tastes."

The art gallery proved to be sheer delight, for the glorious old paintings seemed to glow in the sunshine that poured in through the windows that lined the long outer walls, and the highly polished oak floor and panelled walls shone like glass, whilst the great refectory table in the centre of the room was filled with antique silver that bore the seasoned bloom of well-loved and well-cared-for treasures.

Monsieur Carrilon showed his thirty-five pupils round the gallery, and then left them to do their sketching and painting.

Lucille planted her easel and stool and paints at a good vantage-point; it was by a window at the end of the gallery that overlooked the valley and the lake below, and for a while she was too absorbed to see what Mallery was doing.

Lucille worked away for twenty minutes and then she noticed with surprise that Mallery was still

moving about the gallery, her tackle still not set up and lying stacked neatly in one corner.

But Mallery was not wandering idly about. She was seriously and systematically searching for something, and Lucille began to watch her with growing curiosity. She was longing to ask Mallery what the mystery was, but she knew better than to ask. Mallery could close up like a clam if questioned about her own private and personal affairs.

Suddenly Mallery began to examine an old sword that was lying on the refectory table in its scabbard. She slid the blade out of its sheath and examined it carefully, and then, putting it down quickly on the table, pulled a sketching block and pencil out of her pocket and made a very painstaking sketch of the blade.

Lucille turned her attention to her painting, but half an hour later she observed that Mallery was busy making a sketch of a large painting of an interior of a room in some old house.

Lucille worked on for a while, and then she wandered over to her friend and picked up her sketch-book. "How are you getting on, Mallery?" she inquired. "What's this design in your sketch-book? What is the motive behind it, or is it supposed to be something in the abstract?"

Mallery had risen to her feet when Lucille had approached, and seemed rather furtive about something. She pulled the sketch-book out of Lucille's hands and said: "I'd rather you didn't see that, please. It's . . . well, it's a secret. Please don't ask any questions."

Lucille bit back an angry retort, but thought better of it and remained silent for a few moments. When she did speak again, she spoke of the work that Mallery was doing and carefully kept the conversation off her own efforts.

As the two girls chatted, Mallery carefully put her sketches away in her folder and tied it up securely. She then began to work on an entirely different subject, and Lucille teased her about her secrecy.

"Don't tell anybody about those sketches," pleaded Mallery. "I don't want them discussed or criticised."

When the session had concluded, the students went to the lounge next to the gallery, where afternoon tea was served. As the two friends rested and took their refreshments, a dark-haired girl walked over and introduced herself.

"I'm Norma Billet," she said, her voice dull and toneless.

The two pals introduced themselves and invited Norma to join them for tea, although they were not very impressed with her. Her smooth black hair was beautifully glossy, but her looks were spoiled by her long, thin face, tight-lipped mouth, and narrow eyes. Her lack of expression, both vocally and facially, did nothing to add to her charms.

Norma looked keenly at Mallery and said: "I

saw you sketching something from the armoury department. Are you particularly interested in swords and bayonets?"

Mallery flushed, but quickly hid her feelings. "I was just fooling around," she replied with mock cheerfulness. "I like to sketch a few oddments just by way of 'warming up' before I start serious work."

Norma watched her over the rim of her tea-cup.

"You took quite a long time to 'warm up' today, didn't you?" she said curiously, her keen eyes searching the other girl's face. "May I see the drawings?"

Before either of the girls could stop her, she grabbed Mallery's folder, untied it and spilled the sketches out on to her lap. Mallery rose to her feet in anger and snatched the drawing of the inscription from Norma's hand before the girl had time to really see what was down on paper. Mallery gathered up the remaining sketches and the folder, put the papers away and re-tied the folder securely.

"I'll gladly show you any sketches that you may wish to see if you but ask," she said coldly, "but I prefer to show them to you myself. I don't like people to help themselves."

Norma jumped to her feet in a temper. "Sorry you've been troubled," she cried, and she flounced away from them in a rage.

At dinner that evening the two pals found themselves sitting almost opposite to Norma Billet, but

the dark girl was decidedly cool and only nodded a brief greeting to them. Over coffee, Norma began to hold a very serious conversation with her next-door neighbour, a young man who had been introduced to the pals earlier on as Clavering Pastell.

Clavering was curiously like Norma in appearance. They might almost have been brother and sister. They glanced at the pals from time to time as though they were talking about them. The glances during the close conversation rather gave the show away.

Mallery retired rather early that evening, saying that she had one or two letters to write, but when Lucille followed her up to her room an hour later, she was amazed to find that Mallery was not in the room.

Lucille looked in the wardrobe to see if her dress was hanging there, but was even more surprised to find that Mallery's outdoor clothes were not there either.

She had no idea where Mallery had gone, and so all she could do was to wait anxiously for her to return.

Lucille's anxiety grew as she heard the loud thud of the massive oak front doors being closed, a squeaking and scraping of the old lock as the key was turned. The shooting of bolts set her pacing up and down in a frenzy of worry.

Where had her friend gone to so late at night, and why had she gone out without telling even her best friend?

It was not until twelve o'clock had struck on the town hall clock that Lucille saw a dark figure hurrying in through the gateway that was, fortunately, left open all night. The figure paused under a lamp, and Lucille breathed a sigh of relief as she recognised Mallery.

Mallery looked up at their bedroom window, and Lucille signalled to her with a flashlight. Five minutes later, Mallery had climbed up the ivy-covered drainpipe and in at the first-floor window.

"Wherever have you been, Mallery?" cried Lucille, angry now that her anxiety had been dissolved. "Why don't you tell me what's going on? What are you up to? I've never known you to be so secretive ever before in all the time I've known you."

Mallery sat on the edge of her bed until she got her breath back, and then she said: "The whole thing is so secret, and so important, that I cannot tell anybody the full details, not even you."

Lucille waited in angry silence for her friend to continue.

"I am looking for something," went on Mallery after a slight pause, "that will make a broken life into a new and bright one. I had a hunch about something, but now I know that it is more than a hunch."

Lucille suddenly felt ashamed of herself for her outburst of temper, and said gently to her friend as she looked down at her: "It won't hurt anybody if you tell me the outline of the story. I would be able to help you and I will definitely not divulge any part of your secret to anybody at all. You know that you can trust me."

Mallery remained silent for a few moments, and then she said: "There is a special sword in this castle, and I have just had it proved to me that I have found it. There is a special inscription on the blade, and it contains a clue. The remainder of the clue is mixed up with the interior I was sketching this afternoon. The person most concerned in this matter is staying in Chilbury and I have been to see this person. We have worked out the clues, and now all that remains to be done is to find that room. My friend has found an old book about the castle, and that room is right here under this roof. Somewhere. We must find that room and solve the mystery."

"I'll help you all I can," said Lucille, patting her chum's shoulder. "Don't worry, it will all come out right, whatever it is."

"Today," said Mallery thoughtfully, "I have also discovered that two other people would like to solve that mystery too. They would bring ruin to my friend if they could, and take everything for themselves. Those people are Norma and Clavering. I can't tell you any more yet, Lucille, but we must find that room before they do."

Suddenly the bedroom door was opened and Norma Billet walked into the room, a deep scowl on her face. "What are you doing with a light on at this time of night?" she snapped. "Don't you know

that it is well after midnight? Why aren't you un-
dressed and in bed asleep?"

"I might ask you the same question," replied
Lucille curtly. "We had a few letters to write, then
we read a little, and we were just having a talk
before retiring for the night. We are not at school
now or under school rules; this school of art is
quite a different thing. Our free time is our own,
and you have nothing to do with it."

Norma was plainly taken aback by the stand put up by the girls, and she was at a loss to know how to deal with the situation now.

"I will say nothing this time," she muttered, "but if I catch you two up to any more peculiar moves, I'll report you."

"That goes for you too," snapped Lucille. "Now please leave our room. When we want you in here, we will invite you."

When Norma had left the room, Mallery said: "Now we've got to get moving, and quickly too. I'm sure Norma was listening outside the door."

"We have to find that room tonight," said Lucille, "but how are we going to start? We can't go round the castle from room to room seeking it. That would be impossible."

Mallery gave a little secret smile and produced a shabby book from her pocket. It was the *History of Chilbury Castle*, and contained maps and drawings. Mallery opened it at a page and showed Lucille a drawing. The page showed a drawing of a room. It was identical with the room in the painting. The caption read: THE SMALL DINING-ROOM.

"I caught a glimpse of it this evening," whispered Mallery. "The door was open as I was going out, ostensibly to post a letter. The room is used by Monsieur Carrilon as his private study. We will go and investigate."

Silently the two girls crept down the stairs and into the oak-panelled room, with its wonderful carvings. Mallery produced the two sketches and showed Lucille a special piece of carving on the drawing. The item took the form of a tiny shield bearing the inscription that was also carved on the sword blade.

Mallery and Lucille stared round the room at the various shields that were carved out of the woodwork between each panel, and then began to systematically examine each shield.

"The inscription is on one of these shields," said Mallery, "and somewhere behind the panel, probably in a small secret recess that is opened by a spring, is the other half of the clue."

The minutes ticked by as the girls explored the carvings, working silently and intently. The opening of the door startled them to such an extent that Mallery slipped and fell back against the wall.

Norma Billet and Clavering Pastell burst into the room, followed more sedately by Monsieur Carrilon himself.

"There are the thieves," shouted Norma, pointing excitedly at the two pals. "I told you they were up to no good."

"Not so fast," cried Monsieur Carrilon. "I happen to know a little more about this matter than any of you think. I believe that the young lady here has found the answer to quite a problem."

He stepped up to Mallery, and pointed to the panel behind her. Her fall had accidentally touched a knob, a spring had been set into operation, and the panel had slid back, revealing an elaborate piece of carving hidden away behind it for several generations.

A large yellow package lay in a niche, and Monsieur Carrilon picked it up with a cry of joy. "If my information is correct," he informed them, "here are the deeds of the castle. They will prove definitely and conclusively who the castle really belongs to. Looking at the crest there, I see now that it does not belong to Norma Billet's family. It belongs to the Cane family. Mallery's family. But we shall soon see."

Monsieur Carrilon opened the dusty package and revealed a pile of ancient documents, and he proceeded to go through the papers carefully. The watchers scarcely breathed as he read through the papers.

"It is as I thought," he said, at last. "The Canes are the rightful owners of the castle. It fell into the wrong hands by a trick. You see, besides being an artist, I am also an historian, and when I leased this castle, I read up everything that I could find about it. I read that the castle had fallen into the wrong hands by a trick, and the Billets were not the rightful owners. Norma found out that Mallery was one of the Chilbury Canes. I found that out myself when she enrolled herself as a student here, and Norma has tried to prevent Mallery from finding these papers and the remainder of the proof. Legal proof will be needed, but I do not need that to establish her identity. Just look at this painting."

A small canvas was unrolled and revealed a

painting of a lady standing before the newly revealed carving on the wall. The clothes were Elizabethan, and the lady's face was the image of Mallery's face.

Mallery and Lucille were so engrossed with the painting that they almost missed Norma's next move. The girl snatched at the deeds and rushed to the fire that was still burning in the grate. But Monsieur Carrilon dived towards her and seized the documents and the painting.

"Oh, no you don't," he shouted. "I think you and your half-brother would be well advised to pack your bags and leave these premises immediately. If you ever show yourselves round here again, I shall inform the police."

The following morning, Mallery's father brought his solicitor to the castle and definite identity was proved.

A few weeks later, the new owners of the castle gave a garden party in the grounds for all the students and their parents and friends, and Monsieur Carrilon was the guest of honour, being the tenant of the castle.

Lucille squeezed her friend's hand.

"I see now why you were so keen to enrol here instead of a London art school," she said.

Mallery smiled and replied: "The original clues have been in our family for ages, but we didn't know it. If dad hadn't found that old book in a second-hand shop, we should never have got to the bottom of it."

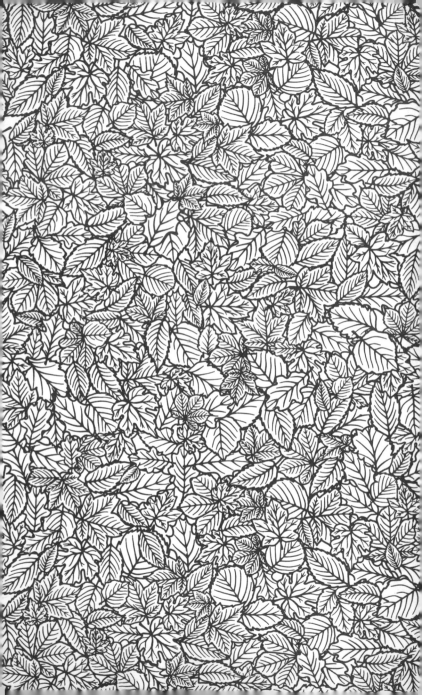